GRACE PALMER

Saved My Life

First edition

ISBN: 979-8-218-30283-2

This book was professionally typeset on Reedsy.
Find out more at reedsy.com

To my family, for your constant support of my dreams
And to teachers everywhere, for encouraging students' love of learning

I

Part I: August

1

Lizzie

It all started on a dark and stormy night . . . I know, I know, that's cliche, but that really is how the whole thing started. It was the night before the first day of my junior year in high school, and it was pouring down rain. Not the nice little shower that's perfect for curling up by the window with a good book, but the kind that makes you scared your roof might blow off. That's probably a tad dramatic, but you get the idea.

The rain was beating down on my window so loudly I could barely think, and I was laying on my loft bed trying to text my best friend, Nolly. We had been friends since that day in fourth grade when I stood up on the cafeteria table and began to tell the whole grade why they should vote for my sister for student council president. I was a feisty little kid and I usually tried to follow the rules, but my big mouth that tended to say whatever was on my mind at the moment usually got me into some pretty big trouble. Needless to say, I was pulled off that lunchroom table before I could finish my passionate campaign speech. In my defense, my sister really would have been a great president (I mean come on, she was promising to get more books for the library and more ice cream for the cafeteria), but, apparently, the fourth-grade lunch monitors did not realize how important school politics were and thought my outburst was completely inappropriate. They were probably more concerned with the fact that I was standing on the lunchroom table, but my little fourth-grade self thought they were against my sister's campaign.

Seeing this as a total failure on my part to support my sister, I sat by myself at the playground after lunch during recess and cried. Nolly came and sat by me on the little butterfly-shaped bench and asked me if I was okay. Like I said, I was offended that the teachers didn't see the importance of the situation and I was worried I let down my sister, but I was also a little embarrassed. Did I go too far? Was everyone in the grade going to think I was weird? Because fourth graders are innocent and open creatures, I told Nolly all of this. She just sat there, listening and nodding. After I finished, we sat there in silence for a little bit until she just said, "I'm sure your sister will win, and she won't be mad at you . . . and I think what you did was pretty cool." Well, that brightened my mood pretty quickly, and my little fourth-grade self got over the cafeteria incident. A few minutes later, Nolly and I were talking about our shared love for ponies, princesses, and popcorn. If you know anything about fourth-grade girls, then you know that that conversation was enough to immediately make us best friends. That weekend, our moms took us to go see a new movie and we ate popcorn and watched the show that involved princesses riding on ponies. Thus, a beautiful friendship was born.

Anyway, that dark and stormy night I was texting her about our plans for the next day when we would officially become upperclassmen. We both had so many plans for things we wanted to do that year, and we were beyond excited for the year to get started. I mean junior year! We both finally had our licenses since Nolly had stopped procrastinating and got hers over the summer, and we had three of our seven classes together, which was more than we had together the past two years.

We were also excited to see each other since we hadn't been able to spend much time together all summer because of camp and work. I camp counseled at Camp Sunshine. I know, I know, stupid name, but really, it's a fun place. There's a water slide, a ropes course, horseback riding, jewelry making, campfires every night, and Bible study every day. While I spent my summer surrounded by crazy, wild, and mostly sweet eleven-year-old girls, Nolly got a job at Oh So Pretty, one of the boutiques in our mall. She worked almost every day, I was gone at camp, and we were both so busy we barely even made time for phone calls. So, needless to say, I was thrilled to get to see my best friend again.

"Liiiizzziieee," I heard my mom call up the stairs.

"Coming," I replied. I quickly texted Nolly that I'd be right back, so we could finish planning our best year yet in just a second. I then ran down the stairs to see what my mom needed. She was sitting at our little, round breakfast table under the stained-glass light fixture in our breakfast nook, working on her computer.

"Hey, Honey," she said when I reached the kitchen. "I have some bad news. I just realized that I have a very important hearing tomorrow, and I won't be able to see you off on your first day of your junior year." My mom was a judge which meant that she was normally pretty busy with bringing justice to the world and keeping the peace and all that jazz, but it also meant that I was used to her being busy.

"It's all good, Mom," I said. "What time is your hearing?" I was fine if she wasn't going to be able to see me in the morning, but she was one of those moms who kept track of every single first. First day of kindergarten? Check. First lost tooth? Check. First sick day home from school? Check, etc., etc., etc. You get the idea. And while I usually found it really nice and sweet, especially since I now have pictures of all of those moments, sometimes she put too much pressure on herself, and I felt bad for her. Missing the first day of junior year would probably be the end of the world for her, so I tried to make sure she wouldn't.

"Well, I have to be at the courthouse at 7:00, and since school doesn't start for you until 8:30, I figured you probably won't be up at 6:30 when I leave," my mom said.

"Just come wake me up right before you leave," I replied. "We can take a picture with me in my pink pajamas and you in your fabulous judge get-up." I said with a laugh.

"Are you sure?" she asked with a slight chuckle.

"Yeah, I don't mind. Getting up early on the first day of school is probably better anyway so I'm not rushed," I replied.

"Okay, thank you so much, Honey," my mom said smiling. "I'll see you bright and early then!"

"Sounds good," I said heading back upstairs to finish texting Nolly.

My mom really was great, even though she was constantly busy trying to balance being a mom and a judge. As a judge, she had to make a lot of really hard decisions, but she always did it in a way that was fair and informed. I'd watched her preside over a few cases and it always just amazed me how she did it. For some of the ones I'd seen, I honestly had no idea what I would have done in her shoes, but she always made good decisions and when she explained her reasoning for her decisions, I was always sure she had made the right ones.

I had considered following in her footsteps, but I figured I would get too caught up in what I thought should happen instead of taking all the evidence into consideration. On the other hand, I didn't really know what else to do. Nothing else really seemed interesting to me. I was too squeamish to be a doctor, too jittery to have a desk job, and too easily annoyed to be a teacher. And that's another reason why junior year was so important. It's when you're supposed to figure out what you're doing with your life. I was hopeful that whatever was going to happen in the upcoming year would help me figure it out.

2

Nolly

"I'm backkk," I got the text from Lizzie just as I had finished putting my room back together. I hadn't cleaned it all summer, and I decided that I probably should since school was starting. It had been a disaster, with clothes, shoes, and makeup scattered everywhere. I had been pretty busy over the summer with theater camp and my job at the local boutique, so cleaning up after myself was the last thing I had wanted to do.

I worked myself nearly to death over the summer at the boutique. At first, I thought I was going to absolutely love it. I love clothes, shoes, and critiquing people's outfits so what better job could I ask for, right? Wrong! The job was so annoying. For one thing, I only got a 5% discount on all the store's merchandise, which was way too little for all the work I was putting in. For another, they told me that the customer was always right. What the heck is that supposed to mean? Even if the customer wants to wear polka dots with plaid, does that mean they are still right? Apparently so. And I wasn't allowed to do any critiquing at all. (Trust me, I tried, and they were not happy with me). To make matters even worse, they expected me to work every day of the week from 10:00-2:00. Starting my day at 10:00 in the morning?? No, thank you. And four hours of grueling work hanging things up, sorting inventory, and worst of all selling people outfits that would never match and never look good on them? It was pure torture. I did get paid a nice $14 an hour (which was good but still not enough in my opinion), and at least I wasn't working at that awful camp Happy Rainbows or wherever it was Lizzie spent her summer, but trust me when I say this, I would much rather have spent the summer sleeping and shopping. Unfortunately, my bank account did not allow that.

I did have theater camp though, which was literally the only thing that got me through this summer. It was two perfect weeks of acting and playing stupid games and pretending that I was a princess of a small island nation and had a gorgeous boyfriend and servants to wait on me. (I was the lead in the play we worked on). It was fabulous. And, to make it even better, my stage boyfriend and I had a stage kiss at the end of the play, and we spent a lot of the camp practicing it to get it just right, if you know what I mean. Unfortunately, my stage boyfriend and I lived like five hours apart, so a relationship wasn't really going to work out, but I didn't consider all the time we spent together at camp a waste in the slightest. Also, I found him on social media when I got back from camp and it turned out he had a girlfriend, so it probably wouldn't have worked out anyway. I wondered if his little girlfriend found out about camp . . .

Anyways, I thought I should probably start the school year off on a clean page, forgetting all of my summer except for theater camp, and I initially thought I should start by getting somewhat organized. It was a nice thought but, I mean, cleaning my room really wasn't going to do much good because it would probably be dirty again by the end of the week. I had never been the most organized person in the world, and I wasn't sure what part of my brain thought I would start now. Also, I was totally dreading going back to school, and cleaning my room felt way too much like preparing for the upcoming year, which was the exact opposite of what I wanted to do. I did not want to go back to school.

While I didn't exactly enjoy my summer, I liked school even less. If I could barely survive a four-hour shift at the boutique every day, how the heck did they expect me to survive an eight-hour school day? Plus, I didn't want to learn anything else about the powerhouse of the cell, factoring polynomials, what year Columbus crossed the ocean blue, or anything at all related to the English language. I was never going to use any of that junk and sometimes I felt like they just taught us the same stupid things over and over again so they could meet the time requirement the state put in place.

The only positive thing about school was that it got me away from the crazy people I lived with (otherwise known as my family). When I was at home, I kept to myself pretty much, trying to avoid my whacked out family as much as humanly possible. You see, both of my parents' jobs weren't exactly legal. Well, actually they were illegal. My parents were smugglers. Of what? I didn't know. They wouldn't tell me. I pretty much ignored them unless I needed something, and they did the same to me.

"Hey, Nolly, take out the trash."

"Fine, Pops, whatever."

"Mom, can I have some money for this new blouse."

"Yeah, fine, take it from the jar on the counter."

And that was the extent of my relationship with my family. It might sound kind of sad, but honestly, it worked for me. So, I guess if I had to pick one silver lining of the school year starting, it would be that I wouldn't have to be around my stupid family. That and the fact that I got to show off my amazing sense of fashion with the new clothes I bought over the summer.

I eventually got around to picking out my outfit for the first day because, even though I was preparing for school, I was expressing my one-of-a-kind fashion sense and I never turned down a chance to do that. I picked out a red V-neck blouse with flouncy sleeves tucked into my new distressed, ripped, black mom jeans. I was going to pair it with my silver ring belt, silver earrings, and white high-top Converse. Perfect.

At some point, I realized that I hadn't responded to Lizzie in a while, so I asked, "What are you wearing tomorrow?"

"TBH, I don't know," she texted back. Lizzie didn't care much for boys or fashion. I, however, cared a great deal about these things. Sometimes I wondered why we were still friends. We literally had nothing in common. I knew we bonded in elementary school over her being a complete weirdo and us both liking typical fourth-grade girl things, but we weren't in fourth grade anymore, and while I grew out of my weirdness, Lizzie . . . well let's just say Lizzie was different. And she has never had a boyfriend, which I'm not saying is a bad thing, but like, we were juniors in high school. Get with the program! Don't get me wrong, there were a few guys she had a crush on, but she was always letting stupid things like school and debate team distract her from them. While I didn't have a boyfriend either, I was at least definitely, without a doubt in the market for one. Everyone said I should get together with Noah, a senior at our school. I thought he liked me, but I wasn't completely sure yet, and to be honest, I just wasn't a fan of him . . .

3

Noah

"Don't forget to pack your baseball gear for practice tomorrow," my dad yelled. "You want to make a good first impression."

"Thanks, Dad!" I yelled back. I was frantically trying to put everything I needed for the first day of school into my bag. I knew I should have done it sooner but, it didn't happen. I had just started to pack my baseball bag, and, like my dad said, it was super important for me to remember everything because we had a new baseball coach this year. Even though I had played baseball in my past three years of high school and I had been on varsity since sophomore year, that didn't mean I would get a good position on the team this year. And I had to get a good position on the team, not only because it was senior year but because I wanted to do it for my mom.

"OK, so I have my school supplies, baseball stuff, school ID, what else do I need?" I said to myself. "Oh, food!" I remembered. Arguably one of the more important items for the day, I ran down the stairs into the kitchen to pack my lunch. My dad was sitting on the couch in the living room watching some sort of game show where they have teams of people do a bunch of physical and mental challenges for some huge amount of money. It was one of my mom's favorite shows and he always watched it when it was on. I don't know if he felt like he had to watch it for her since she couldn't or if he watched it because it reminded him of her, but either way, every Monday night when it came on, he'd watch it.

"Hey, Sport," my dad said as I walked past him.

"Hey!" I said.

"What are you doing?" my dad asked.

"Making my lunch for tomorrow," I replied as I walked into the kitchen. I got out some bread, mayo, cheese, ham, and other sandwich stuff, and began to assemble my lunch. My dad went back to watching TV in the other room.

He was a police officer, so evenings and early mornings were really the only times I got to see him. Otherwise, I was alone. My mom used to be a police officer too. She and my dad met at the academy. One day when they were training my dad was having a difficult time with one of the training exercises and the chief was giving him a hard time. The chief had my mom be the example for the rest of the class (and especially my dad) to watch and figure out how to do the exercise. After my dad got over the initial embarrassment of being shown up by a girl, he realized that the girl was really very pretty, so he asked her to dinner and the rest is history.

They graduated from the academy together, got married, and then became police officers together in the city where we lived. Eventually, they had me, and my mom took a month or two off from work, but she was never really good at sitting still, or so my dad told me. My dad says that he knew she loved me and loved getting to be a mom, but she was just too great of a police officer to be a stay-at-home mom. She was also one of the few women on the police force at the time, and she always wanted to show that women officers could do just as well as their male counterparts. She moved up pretty quickly in the ranks while my dad was happy to stay where he was, but they still got to work together as partners pretty often. They worked really well together too, but their teamwork and my mom's skill only helped them so much. One day, when I was two, she and my dad were responding to a call for armed robbery at one of the local apartment complexes. They got to the apartment just in time to see the crook run out the front door and jump in the getaway car. They chased after him in the squad car for over 10 minutes, until eventually the getaway car lost control and crashed into a tree. My parents got out of their squad car and carefully walked up to the getaway car. Suddenly the door flew open, and the robber jumped out, pointed his gun at my mom, fired it, and ran. My dad was too much in shock to even think about chasing after them. He called an ambulance, but it was too late.

I never really got the chance to know my mom outside of the stories my dad told about her, but I still missed her. My dad made her seem like this amazing woman, and he got this sparkle in his eyes when he talked about her. I knew my dad loved her a lot. We still did things sometimes just because she liked doing them. That was one of the reasons I played baseball. She loved watching baseball and even used a baseball theme to decorate my baby nursery. I loved the sport, of course, but I also did it for her. Whenever I played, I felt like she was cheering me on from up there in Heaven. I also thought that going to my games reminded my dad of her too. They used to go to games together all the time.

Anyway, once my lunch was made and in the fridge, I went back upstairs to double-check everything that was in my bag. I was excited about school the next day, getting to be a senior, and all that. I had senior sunrise the next morning, bright and early at 6:30. I was planning on going with some of the guys I had played baseball with since freshman year. I was looking forward to it and all of the other fun senior traditions that our school does like senior skip day, senior picnic, and senior night for baseball. I just wish my mom could be here for all of it.

4

Meg

"Thanks for making dinner Mom and Dad," I said. My parents had just spent the past hour and a half making a big dinner for the night before the first day of school. It was a tradition we did every year since I started kindergarten. My mom always made fresh mashed potatoes and green beans straight from our garden. She actually picked the potatoes and mashed them, and then she cut, cooked, and seasoned the green beans. My dad made the chicken fried steak and gravy using his signature recipe and secret ingredients that he would never tell me, no matter how hard I begged. Then, we finished the whole meal with an apple pie that I would make completely from scratch. I made the crust with basic ingredients and the filling with apples from our garden, all using my granny's recipe. The whole meal was always so delicious, and I looked forward to it every year.

"Let's dig in!" my dad finally said after we had sat down at the dinner table. After we prayed, we filled our plates with the heavenly goodness.

"Ughh," I moaned, taking a bite. "This is so good. I'm telling y'all it gets better every year."

"I do think we keep outdoing ourselves, don't you Mary?" my dad said with a grin.

"Oh, definitely," my mom agreed. "And I can't wait to taste that pie of yours, Meg," she added, grinning at me.

I loved my parents. I truly believed I had the best parents in the world. They were so sweet and encouraging of everything I did, whether it was baking, 4-H, or anything school related. They could also be silly and stupid at times, which made me love them even more. My mom was a veterinarian, and my dad was a nurse at the hospital. They were such great examples to me of hard work and dedication. They had both worked in their jobs for over 20 years, and I knew it was basic, but I wanted to be like them when I grew up.

It was just me and them at our house ever since my neighbor, Joy, moved off to college. Our family and the family next door to us were really close. I was the only child in my family and Joy was the only child in hers. We spent so much time together that we were practically sisters. If we were home, we were almost always at each other's house. Until she left me to go to more school and train to become a teacher. Or was it a chemist? No wait, it was an accountant. She'd changed her major a hundred times. When Joy left, I was so devastated. She was my best friend, and we did everything together. She took me to all her friends' parties and hangouts, and they always made me feel like I fit in.

When she left, I thought I would have no friends and would be so lonely, but I got a lot closer to my parents, and they really pushed me to get more involved in things at school. I got really into 4-H and made new friends. My parents were so supportive, going to all my stock shows and competitions, and I wouldn't be anywhere close to where I am today without them.

"So, are you excited about tomorrow?" my dad asked in between bites.

"Definitely," I said. "I'm excited mostly about 4-H after school, but I'm excited for school too!" I loved 4-H, the horses especially. I loved riding, feeling the wind in my hair, and feeling the steady rhythm of the horse. There was a ranch about 10 minutes from my house, and almost every day after school, I would drive over there and check on my horse. Her name was Butterscotch, and she was a beautiful caramel color. She had this adorable white spot on her forehead, and she was so, so sweet. She loved being brushed, and she loved sugar cubes even more. She'd done really well in shows in the past, and I was hoping we were finally going to get first place.

Another thing I was excited about doing senior year was raising a goat. Since I'd never raised a goat before, I was excited to try something new. We had a backyard big enough for the goat to have his own pen with some extra room to run around, and I had already set everything up. I was going to go pick up the baby goat in a few weeks, and I couldn't wait. The people I was picking him up from already sent me some pictures, and he was black and white spotted with a big black spot over his left eye. He was adorable! I had already picked out a name too: cuddles! I knew it was really cutesy, but, oh well, if you had seen his pictures, you would get it too.

4-H was going to be great, but I was only kind of excited about the school part of the upcoming year. I enjoyed school, but I would rather be out with the horses or hanging out with my friends or my parents, than sitting, locked up in a classroom. On the bright side, it was the start of my senior year. I was excited about it because it meant I was one step closer to my dream of being a veterinarian. Only one more year of high school, then a few years of undergrad, then finally, vet school! I knew I should probably soak up the moment and enjoy being a senior and make the most of my last year as a kid, but honestly, I felt like senior year was kind of pointless. I didn't really need the classes I was taking (except for the dual credit animal science classes I was taking at the college), and the second half of the year wouldn't even count toward my GPA. I knew that it was my last chance to be a kid, but I had gotten to be a kid for the last seventeen and a half years and I was ready to be done. Not that it hadn't been great, it had been absolutely amazing. I'd had a great childhood; I was just so ready to finally meet my goals. So senior year, I was ready for you . . . if only to check you off and get ready for college.

5

Nolly

"Nolly! Nolly! NOLLY! Get up! It's time to get ready for school!"

And that was how my first day of 11th grade started. I rolled (literally) out of bed and put on my carefully picked out outfit, complete with my white high tops and silver belt.

"Knock, knock, knock," I heard on my door.

"Come in," I said groggily, very much still waking up.

"Nolly," my brother, Luke, said. "I leave in 15 minutes, and if you are not ready to go by then, you're taking the bus."

I stared at him in shock. First off, very confused because, didn't I spend a good part of my summer doing all that stupid stuff for driver's ed so that I wouldn't be put into situations like these? That's when I remembered: my parents had borrowed my car to go out of town. Where did they go? I had no idea, but the fact that they had taken my car, making my only mode of transportation to school my brother who was leaving in 15 minutes was a huge problem.

"15 minutes?" I asked Luke, beginning to panic. "It takes me thirty minutes to do my hair and makeup alone. What about breakfast and packing my backpack?" This could not be happening. No way my school year was starting off like this. I needed time to look good. I had a reputation to uphold, and I could not, repeat could not, show up to school on the first day with only 15 minutes of hair and makeup. And there was definitely no way I was taking the bus. Maybe my brother would wait for me?

"Well, looks like you're taking the bus," Luke said as he headed out of my room. I glowered after him. I could not believe he was going to make me do that. I knew it was not that big of a deal to most people, but, to me, it may as well have been torture. I mean the bus driver kept all the windows open, so it would always mess up my hair, the bus stank so much that it masked the smell of my perfume, and there was always gross stuff on the seats that would ruin my clothes! I couldn't stand it! I had done it once before, and never again. I had nightmares about it for weeks where yellow school buses with fangs chased after me and ate me! It was truly traumatizing.

After pouting for about ten minutes, I decided to call Lizzie and ask her to take me to school. That was my last hope. As I walked to my bathroom, and began putting on my makeup, Lizzie picked up the phone. "Hey, I need a ride," I said. Lizzie understood my situation: the fact that I needed my beauty time in the morning and that I was never going to ride the bus if there was anything I could do to avoid it, so she happily said she would be at my house in forty-five minutes. With that, I hung up and began making myself pretty much the most beautiful girl at school. Like I said, I had a reputation to uphold.

6

Noah

"She really is the most beautiful girl in school," I thought to myself as we drove past Nolly's house on the way to school.

"Are you going to finally ask her to Homecoming, Noah?" asked Trevor, my best friend, as though he could read my thoughts. Either that or he just noticed me looking wistfully at her house.

"I don't know," I replied. "Remember that time in sophomore year when I tried to ask her to the Halloween dance, and I ended up asking her if she had a wiener dog instead? That was so embarrassing!"

"Oh yeah, Dude," Trevor said with a laugh. "That was real bad. But that was two years ago, maybe you're better at talking to girls now."

"I don't know," I repeated. "Besides, there is a big fundraiser going on at the Children's hospital that night I don't want to miss."

Trevor stared at me blankly. "Dude, you cannot miss your senior homecoming dance for some fundraiser at the hospital!"

Trevor knew that I loved to volunteer at the children's hospital, since I wanted to be a doctor there when I grew up. I spent pretty much all my free time there. But this time, Trevor was adamant.

"C'mon, Noah! You have to go!" he said.

"It's not even for a couple of months, Trevor. Don't get so fired up!" I replied.

"Fine," he said.

Trevor really did mean well, it's just sometimes he got really stubborn. Trevor and I had been friends since freshman year when we were the only two freshmen on JV. We got along pretty well, but sometimes Trevor was so stubborn. He was good for me though because he made sure I did all the fun high school things, got involved with people and events, and apparently would force me to go to my senior homecoming.

We got to the school just as the sun was starting to rise. That was another thing that was Trevor's doing: us going to senior sunrise. I would have been fine just sleeping in, but he really wanted to go, and he didn't want to go by himself. I felt bad for him, so I decided to go. Plus, he needed a ride.

I parked my truck, and we climbed out. Looking around, I saw a table with donuts and orange juice, a place to write notes to our future selves that would be given back at the end of the year, a little photo booth complete with props, and a bunch of girls in all different colors of pajama pants.

After a quick glance, I realized that the majority of people at the sunrise were girls. Great.

Trevor dragged me over to go write letters to our future selves, then we went and got donuts and juice.

"See man," Trevor said, biting into his strawberry glazed donut with sprinkles. "Isn't this great?"

"That's one way of putting it," I replied. Trevor looked like I had just said I thought his puppy was ugly.

"You're not having fun?" he asked, sadly.

"No, no, no, Trevor, I am," I reassured him. "Thanks for dragging me to come do this." That got him smiling. And it was true. The donuts were good, the letter writing was a cool idea, and the sunrise actually was pretty. I was thankful I got to start off senior year like this.

7

Lizzie

"Bye, Dad!" I said as I walked out of the door for the first day of school.

"Bye, Hon," he said. "Have a great day and don't get sent to the principal's office."

"Ha, ha," I said, with a smile, closing the door and heading for my car. That was a running joke of his since my first day of sixth grade when I actually did get sent to the principal's office.

I had gotten lost trying to find my second period. The bell had already rung, and I was walking around the halls trying to find someone to ask about where my class was and apparently, I found the wrong person. When I went up to them, they got mad at me for pretty much everything: for being in the hallway after the bell had rung, for wearing a skirt that was too short (even though it went just past my fingertips), and for "talking back" when I tried to explain that I was lost and that I thought my skirt was in dress code. She escorted me (rather roughly I might add) all the way to my assistant principal's office. Thankfully, the AP agreed with me that my skirt was fine and was kind enough to explain where my second period class was.

When I got home from school that day, I told my parents I had gone to the principal's office. They were horrified for a minute until I told them what happened. Since then, every first day of school my dad gives me that friendly reminder to not repeat my first day of sixth grade. I'm starting to think it's his favorite thing about back-to-school.

Anyways, I got in my car and drove over to Nolly's house to pick her up. I texted her and told her I was there and then waited for ten minutes. She was my best friend, but sometimes she could be a little annoying when she didn't have her stuff together. I didn't mind picking her up, but I had told her when I would be at her house, and I thought it was a little inconsiderate that she wasn't ready.

When she finally got in my car, she plopped down in the passenger seat with a huff. "It's been a crazy morning," she said dramatically. "First, my brother couldn't give me a ride, then I spilled perfume all over my shirt and had to change my entire outfit, then I found out we had no good breakfast food so I'm absolutely starving."

"Good to see you too Nolly," I said with a smile. Nolly's dramatic nature made me laugh. "Do you want a protein bar? I have some in the console." She got her protein bar, and we spent the rest of the quick car ride to school catching up on each other's summers.

We drove through the streets of beautiful Revere, Massachusetts, and I could feel the hint of fall in the air. It wasn't quite there yet, but it was coming. The trees were still green, but pretty soon they would all be gorgeous shades of red and orange. We got to school, parked, and began walking towards the building with five minutes to spare.

The school was a big red-ish building with lots of windows and the words "Revere High School" in big bold letters on the side. We walked towards the front entrance and the huge statue of Paul Revere that stood in front of it. If you haven't guessed, he was a pretty big deal around here. I mean, our school and the whole town were named after him. We'd all heard *The Midnight Ride of Paul Revere* at least a hundred times throughout our school years and we even had a reenactment of the whole thing every summer. It was a funny, crazy, and not at all historically accurate tradition.

Anyways, as Nolly continued the discussion we were having in the car about her various summer romances (yes, she had multiple). I looked around the entryway and saw the principle, standing there and shaking everyone's hand. Our principal, Mr. McCarson, was super friendly and was actually really involved with the students. He would always compete in the contests that we had at pep rallies, and he always participated in the spirit dress up days.

"Hello, Lizzie and Nolly!" he said. "Ready for a great year?"

"Yes, sir!" I replied.

Nolly wasn't focusing, probably off in boy dream land or wherever it is that she goes, so I nudged her in the side, to which she said, "What? Oh, yes, I am!" And we hurried away.

"Nolly," I teased. "What were you doing back there?"

"Oh! There was this really nice-looking boy looking at me," she trailed off.

"Oh, goodness," I replied. "What am I going to do with you?" she grinned sheepishly. "Barely five minutes into the new year and you've already got your eyes on another boy."

"It's not my fault I'm gorgeous," she said, flipping her hair. "Plus, he was the one looking at me."

"Whatever you say," I said with a laugh, right as the first bell rang.

"C'mon let's go or we'll be late to class," I said.

"So will all these other people!" Nolly replied, motioning to the crowds around us.

"Yeah, but we need to make a good first impression, so let's go."

We walked briskly through the halls and sat down in our first period Advanced English class just as the second bell rang. I gave Nolly a pointed look, and she rolled her eyes at me. The teacher walked in, introduced herself as Ms. Perkins, and began talking about what supplies we would need for class. I pulled out my notebook and began writing everything down. I then glanced over at Nolly, and it looked like she was ready to fall asleep. I shook my head, laughing, and went back to my notes.

Suddenly, Ms. Perkins' phone rang. After she answered it, she said, "Meg Martin, you're needed in the front office. They said you can take your things with you."

A girl sitting in the back stood up, picked up her backpack, and left the room. School had started 15 minutes ago. Was someone already in trouble? Or was something else going on?

8

Meg

What?! Come to the office? What did I do? Did I do anything? All of these thoughts popped into my head as soon as soon as Ms. Perkins told me I was needed in the front office. The only other people that I had seen sent to the front office were people who usually got in trouble. But I wasn't like that. I had never been to the principal's office.

Now, I was sitting in English with a whole bunch of kids I barely knew staring at me, some confused, some repulsed, and some in awe. I guess everyone was thinking what I was thinking: that either I was in trouble or something weird was happening. The only people who weren't staring at me were the ones who were asleep (which was quite a few).

"Go on now, Meg," said Ms. Perkins, bringing me out of my panic for a moment. "I'm sure they just want to talk to you about your schedule or something." I got up and walked out of the class slowly. As soon as I was out the door, the room erupted into whispers behind me.

Oh great, I thought. Now everyone knows me as the kid who

went to the principal's office on the first day of school. This was a terrible start to my senior year. As I walked down the hall, I grew more and more panicked. I couldn't think of anything I had done wrong, and I knew there was no problem with my schedule, so what could it be?

I was the quiet, sweet kid who didn't really talk, let alone go to the principal's office. I was so consumed by my thoughts that I didn't realize where I was going, and I walked right into another kid in the hallway. I looked up and realized that it wasn't just "another kid." It was Noah.

"Oh, I'm sorry," he said, and walked away. Now, my heart was beating even faster.

Noah and I used to be really close. Our freshman year of high school, we had almost our entire schedule together, except when I had ag, he had baseball. We became really good friends, and he asked me to go to homecoming. We went together, and we had so much fun dancing with each other all night long. Our relationship (whether it was a friendship or more than that I was never really sure) continued through the year and into the summer. We hung out at the pool, went to the beach, and even got jobs lifeguarding together.

But then, sophomore year came. We didn't have any classes together and eventually just grew apart and stopped talking. Not because of anything either of us did, just because that's how life happened. I really hadn't seen him around much since then, but I guess today was already out of the ordinary. It was just one of those days.

I continued on to the principal's office while trying to put the boy out of my head. I thought I would have to wait when I got there, but the secretary looked at me sadly and said to go right in. "What is going on?" I thought. "Why did the secretary look so sad? Maybe she just had a rough morning?"

I walked into the principal's office, and, to my surprise, there was another man in there too. He was wearing black sunglasses and a black suit. "Hello, Meg," the principal said calmly. "Please, sit down." This was weird. He didn't seem mad or anything, just sad.

"This is Agent Whitefield," the principal continued.

"Agent?" I asked in a shaky, quiet voice.

"Yes," started the principal, but Whitefield cut in.

"Maybe I better explain. You see Meg, I work for a special branch of the government that recruits teenagers, some of the brightest minds, to fight crime. You are being recruited for this team."

"What?" I thought. "Me?" I whispered. This was not something I would be good at or had any desire to do. Why on earth would they pick me? "W . . . W . . . Why?" I asked.

"Well, um . . ." the agent started. "There is no easy way to put this Meg, but . . . your parents are gone. They died in a car crash this morning."

With that one sentence, my world crashed, and I broke down along with it.

9

Noah

I was in my first period class bored out of my mind. The teacher was going on and on about rules and expectations. I think that, as seniors, we should have known them all by now. I mean they were important and all that, but we'd heard them at the beginning of school for the past three years. If they hadn't sunk in by now, they weren't going to.

Desperately trying to stay awake, I asked to go to the bathroom. Not that I really needed to, I just felt like falling asleep on the first day would give a bad impression, not to mention that it's just rude. As I took my time walking to the restroom, not wanting to get back to class too quickly, I bumped into a girl. "Oh, I'm sorry," I apologized. She nodded and walked away, barely looking me in the face.

Now, normally, I would have thought nothing of it. But this girl was beautiful. And familiar. She had hair the color of chocolate and eyes the color of the sky. And then I remembered who she was: Meg! Meg Martin! We had been best friends freshman year. We had almost all of our classes together. We first started being friends in our biology class when we had to dissect a frog.

Our teacher had thought it would be a fun way to start the year, so the second week of school she paired all of us up and gave us a frog to take apart. Meg was excited at first because she wanted to be a vet, so she thought it would be a good experience for her. When we started to take the frog apart, though, she got upset. I remember she said that she wanted to help animals, to heal and put them back together instead of taking them apart. Since she was so upset, I finished dissecting the frog for both of us.

After that, we became really great friends. We did all sorts of things together and became so close. I really wanted to ask her out, but I was so scared that we would date then have a messy break up and never talk again, like I saw so many other freshmen couples doing. Plus, we were happy just being friends. Then, I don't know what happened, but we just kind of stopped being friends. I should have asked her out while I had the chance, but we just grew apart without either of us meaning to.

I hadn't seen her in a while, but we followed each other on social media, and she seemed like she was doing good. Right now, though, she looked terrified. "I wonder why," I thought. Meg was a little timid sometimes, and I remembered her being the kind of girl who wore her heart on her sleeve. I was a little worried about her, though. She had scurried away without even saying anything to me. And the expression on her face. What was wrong with her? Was she okay? She seemed scared.

I only got that scared when I got in trouble with my dad. Maybe that's what it was: she was in trouble, or at least thought she was. Meg wasn't the kind of girl to get in trouble, but she definitely was the type of person who would think she was in trouble when she knew she did nothing wrong. "Maybe I'll text her later," I thought. It was our last year at school after all, probably the last chance we'd have to be friends again.

As I continued on to the bathroom, I saw Nolly going into the library. I remembered what Trevor had said to me on the way to school that morning about finally, maybe asking her to homecoming. He would want me to go follow her into the library and talk to her, but there was no way I was doing that. And I did have to go back to class at some point. I settled with waving to her, but I don't think she noticed me because she didn't wave back . . . or maybe she did notice me and just didn't want to wave back. That was a little depressing.

Nolly was pretty, sassy, funny, and I had liked her since we had worked on a theater production together my sophomore year. That year, the theater department at our school had put on a play that raised money for the children's hospital, so I had decided to help out. Because Nolly was only a freshman, she had a small acting part and mostly worked on the set, which was what I was mainly working on. We worked on it together for about a month, and we had a lot of fun, but once the play was over, so was our friendship.

I kept trying to get up my nerve to ask her out, but it seemed like she almost always had a boyfriend, which made me think that maybe she wasn't as great of a person as I thought she was. She seemed like she might be a player. But Meg was the opposite of that. She was beautiful, quiet, and kind . . . "Get ahold of yourself." I thought. "Enough about girls. You don't even know if you'll see Meg this year. You need to get back to class." And I did. I turned around and went right back to class without even going to the bathroom.

10

Nolly

So, I did see Noah on my way to the library. He looked off in another world (one of the many, many things I didn't like about him), so I was surprised when he waved to me. I didn't even think he had noticed me, but then again, I did look good today (like I did every day, of course). I pretended not to notice his little wave because, well, honestly, I didn't want to talk to him.

And the truth was, I was going to the library to meet up with another boy. Call me crazy, but I was pretty popular at my school, and there were lots of boys who wanted a chance with me. I would never admit my mid-class meet-up to Lizzie, though. She would kill me. She was basically a goodie two-shoes and I was basically . . .not.

I had texted the boy, Jake, the night before and we had agreed to meet in the library during first period. Jake and I had a class together last year, so we knew each other, and we had texted on and off all summer, so I decided why not give it a shot? Also, throughout my past two years at high school, I had learned that you could never wait for a guy to ask you out. You just had to do it yourself because, if you didn't, you might be waiting forever. Lizzie would completely disagree with me on this too, saying that I should just be patient and see how it all played out, but since when have I listened to her? Even in elementary school, she would tell me I shouldn't do things, and I would do them anyways, get in trouble, and she would tell me "I told you so." I was in trouble a lot, but at least I had fun.

One time, in middle school, I wanted to skip school and go to the mall. Lizzie, of course, told me not to, begged me even. I, of course, did it anyway. I had a great time too. I had saved up some money that I had gotten for my birthday a month before, and I bought a new blouse. Then, I bought a pretzel and sat on one of the benches to eat it. Unfortunately, that's when one of my teachers noticed me. What was she doing at the mall? What a great question. According to her, she'd had a doctor's appointment that morning and was grabbing lunch before heading back to school. I didn't believe her and told her she was basically skipping school too, which made her even more mad. She drove me back to school in her car, and I ended up getting in-school suspension for the rest of the week. That part was not pretty, but I would say it was well worth it. Lizzie was very, very mad at me though. I remember thinking that I wasn't sure if she was more mad that I broke the rules or that I would be in ISS for the rest of the week, and she wouldn't have her best friend to sit with at lunch.

Anyways, I walked into the library, grabbed a book off the shelf and went into the back corner where I saw Jake sitting. "Hey, Gorgeous," he said, as I sat down. All in all, he was definitely better than Noah, but Jake was not the one for me. We talked for about 15 minutes before we decided to get back to class. It was a nice conversation, but it started to get a little boring. And while Jake did have nice, lush black hair and a cute little dimple, the only sport he played was golf, which I thought was just plain stupid. Like how is it even a sport? You try to hit a teeny-tiny ball into a teeny-tiny hole that you can't even see? It sounded pretty dumb to me. I definitely did not want a golf boyfriend. I checked out the book I had randomly grabbed (*The story of Alfred the Brave*) so it would look like I had actually gone to the library, went to the bathroom to apply a coat of lip gloss, and headed back to class.

By the time I had gotten back to class, the teacher had finished talking and was letting the class talk amongst themselves. As I was walking to my seat, I saw the teacher glance at me quizzically, but, thankfully, she didn't say anything. I guess 20 minutes was a little long to be in the library. I sat down and Lizzie started asking me questions about why it took me so long, did I really go to the library, etc., etc. Sometimes, I wondered why I was even friends with that girl.

11

Lizzie

"What took you so long?" I asked. "You were gone for almost half the class. You missed, well, pretty much everything." I had written everything down in my notebook, so of course, and I would share it with her, but still, what look her so long?

"I was trying to find a good book," Nolly said. "You know how long that takes." I did know how long that took. I would spend hours in the library looking for books, and I would usually only find one that I thought would be good. But that was me, not Nolly. Nolly hated reading. She considered reading anything other than a magazine a waste of time.

Still suspicious, I asked, "So, did you find a good book? Let me see it." She looked a little frustrated, and maybe something else, as she handed me the book. Apprehensive? Annoyed? I couldn't tell. I looked at the book cover. It had a jellyfish on it. *Alfred the Brave?* I asked. There was no way Nolly would read a book about a brave jellyfish. For one, it looked like one of those chapter books for beginning readers, which wouldn't even make sense for her to read. For another, it looked like one of those books that teaches a moral lesson, which I'm pretty sure Nolly would hate reading.

"The librarian recommended it," Nolly said, shrugging. "She said we would read it this year because it's all about figurative language. Stop pushing me all right? I just wanted to get ahead!"

"Okay, okay!" I said, as the bell rang. All I could think about, however, was that there was no way Nolly was telling the truth. Nolly never wanted to get ahead, and, while Nolly wasn't there in class when the teacher mentioned the books we would read this year, I was. And *Alfred the Brave* wasn't one of them.

* * *

As I walked to my advanced math class, a class Nolly and I didn't share, I thought about how Nolly had lied to me so easily. "We're supposed to be friends," I thought. We were so different, but opposites are supposed to attract. Our friendship, even though it didn't really make sense, had always worked before, so why did it feel like we were really growing apart lately?

We had spent the entire summer apart, which I thought would be good for us. We had gotten into a pretty big disagreement at the end of last school year, so I thought a little distance between us might be good. Then when school started back, I was hoping we could pick up our friendship from where we left off, before our big fight.

I had gotten mad at Nolly because she had lied to me about missing my birthday dinner. I was having dinner with a few friends to celebrate my sixteenth birthday, but Nolly called me a few hours before it was supposed to start saying that she was sick. She really sounded sick too. She told me she wasn't going to make it to my party, and, while I was upset she wouldn't be there, I understood. You can't really control when you get sick, after all.

Anyways, I decided to go pick up some of her favorite soup and bring it by her house. When I got there, I knocked on the door, but no one answered so I let myself in. I went upstairs to her room and knocked on her bedroom door. She opened it, and her jaw dropped when she saw me. I was shocked too because she did not look sick in the slightest. She was wearing a tight, skimpy orange-red dress that had a plunging neckline and barely covered her butt. She was wearing bright red lipstick, long dangly earrings, and high heels. "What are you wearing?" I had asked her, totally confused. She didn't even try to lie that time. She told me that her ex-boyfriend was having a party, and he invited her, and she was going. With that, she grabbed her keys and left. I stood there holding the soup I had brought for her, completely shocked and hurt.

After that night, I avoided her for a while. Eventually, the topic came up and we had a full-on screaming match about it, which ended in both of us crying. It was not pretty, and we both decided that a summer where we didn't talk a whole lot might be good for us. Now though, I'm not sure if even time can fix all the problems in our friendship.

As I sat down in my math class, I listened to the conversation going on around me, trying to take my mind off of Nolly. Surprisingly, a lot of it was about that Meg girl that had been called to the office this morning. News travels fast in high school, and the rumors were flying. After she was called in, she didn't come back to class, but I had thought nothing of it. Apparently, the other kids thought it was a big deal. One kid said he thought she was being shipped off to a fancy private school. Another kid said that she was sure seeing Meg on the bus that morning was the last time they would ever see her.

I didn't really know Meg; we had one class together the year before, but that was all. These rumors we're ridiculous though, so I stopped listening. Leave it up to a classroom full of bored teenagers to make something out of nothing. People just need some sort of drama to keep them entertained. Just as I was opening my notebook, something someone said caught my attention. One kid said that he saw her with a guy wearing a suit and sunglasses and carrying a briefcase, and he thinks it was a government agent who was recruiting Meg to be a spy.

Normally, I would think that would be ridiculous as well. But I had seen the guy he was talking about in the office on the way into school. He did have a briefcase, sunglasses, and a suit, and I could see him being a government agent. He definitely looked official. Could the kid be right? Could he be a government agent? If so, was Meg going to be a spy? "No," I said to myself. "That's crazy. There's no way that's true." Looks like I was just another once of those drama-starved high school kids who's willing to believe anything she hears.

12

Meg

At first, I was in absolute shock. I didn't know what was going on. The world started spinning, and all I heard was water in my ears. Then, everything got blurry as my eyes filled with tears. I didn't bawl or throw myself on the ground. I just sat there staring at nothing, tears rolling down my face and falling into my lap.

One thing kept running through my head: *Your parents are gone. They died in a car crash.* I knew the agent and the principal were both staring at me, at a loss for what to do or say. What are you supposed to do in a situation like this? We sat in silence for what felt like forever and just one second at the same time.

Eventually, the agent said something, but I didn't hear. It was like I was in a different world, like the part of me that understood things and made me keep moving had died right along with my parents. The agent placed a hand on my shoulder. Said something else I didn't hear. He then opened the door to the office and gestured for me to come. I stood up and followed the agent out the door. I seemed to have no control over my body. That part of me had died, too.

We walked to a black sedan, and I got in and buckled my seat-belt. Following directions and habits that had been ingrained in me forever were about the only things my brain could handle. My mind was blank as the agent started the car and drove off. Parents. Car. Agent. Crash. Government. Dead. Special branch.

My mind began to whirl as it started to process everything the agent had said in the office. My parents were gone, but what was happening to me? Why did a government agent tell me about my parents, and not a policeman or hospital person? What had he said at the beginning? A special government branch? I could only remember bits and pieces of the conversation, and what I did remember was swirling around in my head so fast I could barely make a coherent thought.

I was a strange mixture of panic and numbness. I felt confused and frozen. Terrified and sad. My parents were gone? Really? I was supposed to stop crime? Me? Without my parents' support? Was that what he actually said? Or was I so shocked I was making everything up? My brain was still confused, but my body knew what to do. I had to get out, make this all go away. This wasn't real, this couldn't be happening. I had to leave. I needed to.

At the next red light, I unbuckled, pulled open the car door, jumped out, and ran across an open field on the side of the road. Away from the government. Away from being an orphan. Away from everything. Maybe if I ran far enough, it would all disappear. Maybe, any second now, I would wake up and it would all be a dream. That had to happen because there was no way this wasn't a nightmare. I ran as fast as I could, hearing the agent yelling after me as I did. Not caring, I kept going. I didn't make it very far. Tears were streaming from my eyes, making it hard to see. I tripped over a rock, hit my head on the ground, and blacked out.

* * *

When I woke up, I was completely disoriented. "Where am I? This isn't my room . . . What's going on?" I thought. I looked around. I was in a small room with light blue walls, a small white desk, a navy nightstand, and the twin-sized white bed I was sitting in. The walls were bare. There were no family pictures on the desk, no horse poster on the wall, and no fuzzy green blanket at the foot of the bed. Where was I?

"Mom?" I cried out. Then, I was submerged in a wave of reality. Everything that happened the day before hit me. My parents were gone and never coming back. I buried my head in my pillow and screamed and cried until I ran out of tears. I lay there for hours, with no desire to get up. I didn't want to do anything other than cry in a world without my parents. And on top of them being gone, I was in a strange place with no idea what was going to happen to me next. It was too much for me to handle. I lay in the bed, staring at the ceiling, for almost the entire day.

Eventually, I heard a knock at the door. I didn't answer, but whoever it was came in anyway. "Hey," she said. I said nothing. Who was this person, barging into my room? Didn't they know I didn't want anything to do with anyone or anything right now? I just wanted to lie here and either pretend nothing was happening and stare at the ceiling or cry until I became too dehydrated to cry anymore.

The girl grabbed a chair and pulled it up to my bed. And she sat there. She didn't say or do anything. She just sat there. She had dirty blonde hair, light blue eyes, and a kind smile. I stared at her through puffy, red eyes and asked, "What . . . What are you d-doing?" It started out as a yell. I wanted to yell. At her, at the people who crashed into my parents, at anything. I was so angry. But it ended with a voice crack and a whimper. I wanted to cry again. I was just so, so depressed.

"Nothing," she replied to my question. "I just wanted to be here for you, you know, if you need to talk or vent or if you just don't want to be alone." I looked at her for a second, surprised. And then, through my tears, I told her everything. For some reason, I opened up to this stranger. Maybe because I couldn't bear the weight alone. Maybe because I just needed to process everything out loud. Or maybe there was just something so kind and gentle about her that I knew she really would listen and do what she could to help me.

She listened and nodded the whole time, and I could tell that she really cared. I told her all my feelings, doubts, fears, and everything else going on inside. When I was finished, she said, "I am so proud of you." I started crying again. "You are so brave, and I am so, so sorry about your parents. My parents died when I was your age too, so I remember what you are going through. It feels like your world is ending, and everything is crashing down around you. It feels like you will never feel happy again and things will never get better. You're confused, sad, scared, and lonely." I nodded. She had just described exactly what I was feeling. "But, I promise, eventually, things will get better. It will take time, and things won't ever be the same, but they will get better. I know that doesn't really help much right now, but I'm here for you if you need anything." I smiled at her, or tried to at least, through my tears. She had said exactly what I needed to hear.

"Who are you?" I asked her. "I'm Katherine," she replied.

"But everyone calls me Kat. I was recruited just like you, right after my parents died. It was hard but I made it. And so will you."

"Thank you," I said, meaning it. Kat told me she had made some food, and it was in the fridge in the main room. I told her I wasn't hungry and that I'd eat later. She then left, after making sure I was okay with being alone.

I wasn't better, actually very far from it. But talking with Kat did help me, if only the tiniest bit. I had so many questions about this new life I was just thrust into, like what had Kat meant when she said she was *recruited just like me*? I needed to figure out and adjust to this new life, but that was not nearly as important as figuring out how to navigate life in general without my parents. My emotions and thoughts and everything inside of me was still so jumbled that I went back to sleep without eating whatever it was that Kat had made.

Kat came by the next day to check on me again. When she came in, I was in the same spot she had left me in, lying in the bed staring at the ceiling. "How are you doing today?" she asked.

"I don't know how to answer that question," I said honestly, keeping my eyes on the ceiling. She gave me a sad smile.

"I get it," she replied. "Everything's too confused and mixed up to really make sense." I nodded.

She waited a few seconds then said, "Look, I know you probably don't want to get out of bed . . ." I nodded again. "But would you be okay with getting up for a few minutes to eat something. It will be good for you."

I slowly sat up, looking at her. Come to think of it, I was hungry. Really hungry, but because of everything else that had happened, I hadn't paid much attention to the growing hunger in my stomach. I nodded again. "Great, thank you," Kat said warmly.

I got out of bed, and she walked me out of the bedroom and into another room. The walls in the room were painted the same light blue color as the bedroom. There was a grey couch facing a TV with a small white table in between. There was also a kitchen with all the appliances and a little bar with white bar stools.

Kat had me sit down on the couch while she went to get the food. She handed it to me, and I started eating right away. It was so good. It was some sort of soup with white cream, little dumplings, and vegetables. While I ate, Kat told me about herself, even though I hadn't asked. It was nice though. It was distracting. She loved the color green. She loved watching movies. She loved karate. She hated pickles. She hated wearing brown. She hated taking notes. She was neutral about pasta. It was fun listening to her talk.

After I finished, she helped me get back in bed and I fell right asleep. The next day, we repeated the routine, except this time, she asked me to take a shower. She showed me the bathroom and explained how the shower handles worked. She waited for me in the main room while I cleaned up. Standing under the running water felt so good. It felt like I could rinse off all my problems and feelings and watch them go down the drain. If only it was that easy. At least I was clean.

After the shower, Kat helped me back to my bed, which had fresh sheets on it. I climbed in and again fell right asleep. For the next two weeks, that was the routine. Kat would come in and I would eat and shower, but each day I would do more, eventually getting up at the beginning of the day, showering and eating breakfast. Then, I would read, watch TV, color or paint, or do some of the other activities Kat had left for me. Next, I'd eat lunch then take a nap. When I woke up, I would make my own dinner, then shower and go to bed.

With each passing day, the pain got easier to deal with. It didn't go away, not at all, but I got used to it and I learned that I would be able to live without my parents, even if it would be hard.

After two weeks had passed, Kat told me she had something important to talk to me about. "Are you ready?" she asked. I was pretty sure the important thing she had to talk to me about was the reason why I was there, in that little blue apartment. Was I ready? I hadn't forgotten about the agent who brought me here and everything he said about being in a special branch of the government. But was I ready to know more? Was I ready to start what seemed to be a new life?

"I don't know," I told Kat honestly. "But, tell me anyway."

"Okay," she said, with a deep breath.

"Before I start, I just want to say how proud I am of you. You've gone through so much and you're still here, still going. You decided to not let the grief defeat you, and I'm just so impressed watching you overcome everything. I think you're ready for anything life throws at you."

"Thank you, Kat," I replied with tears in my eyes. "I couldn't have done this without you." She smiled at me, then reached into her bag and pulled out a folder. She handed it to me, and I opened it, immediately overwhelmed by the amount of information inside. I looked up at Kat without even reading a page, my eyes begging her for answers.

Finally, she told me what in the world was going on. "So, Meg," Kat started. "You are here because you are being recruited by a branch of the government called the Keepers.

This branch is a group of smart, intuitive kids who escape hardship at home by becoming a Keeper. Everyone in this branch, including myself, is or was a kid whose parents had died, were abusive, or were addicts. The people who join this program are recruited because the recruiters believe that them joining the program would benefit them and save them from trauma at home. Because of how most of these kids have grown up, they are stronger, smarter, and more cunning than most adults. Also, kids in general have sharper minds and usually see the simple solutions that adults miss. What's more: criminals under-estimate them, which makes them ideal spies."

I nodded along as Kat explained. Everything she said made perfect sense and no sense at the same time. It was a lot to absorb. As Kat continued to explain what kinds of things the kids in the program did, I thought about something she had said. *Because of how most of these kids have grown up, they are stronger, smarter, and more cunning than most adults.* Because of how these kids had grown up. With parents who were never there. With parents who hit them. With parents who were too hungover to take care of them. These kids had to be strong and cunning if they wanted to survive. That's why they were good spies. But that wasn't me. I hadn't grown up like that. I wasn't cunning or smart or strong. I couldn't be a spy.

"Do you have any questions, Meg," Kat asked, finishing her spiel and pulling me out of my thoughts. "I know this can be a lot to take in."

"I can't do this, Kat," I told her. "This isn't me. I didn't grow up like the rest of these people. I had a comfortable life. I worked hard, but I didn't have people hit me or neglect me. I didn't have some huge trial in my childhood that made me stronger."

"What would you call what you're going through right now?" Kat asked me quietly.

My parents died. It had totally rocked my world. It crushed me, but Kat was right. It had made me stronger and tougher. I was still struggling with it, but it was making me stronger every day. Maybe I could do this. Kat saw something in me. Maybe I just needed to see it in myself.

"I know this is a lot to handle," Kat said. "You can have as much time as you need to decide, and if you don't want to do it at all, that's totally fine. We will figure something out."

I didn't need time. My mind was made up. My parents were gone. I had no other relatives, no siblings, cousins, aunts, uncles, grandparents. No one. I had to do this.

"I want to do it," I said. "I want to be a spy."

"I knew that's what you would say," Kat said, smiling. "Training starts tomorrow."

She wasn't kidding. For the next couple months, I trained all day, every day. I learned things like observation, reading a crime scene, tracking people down and other skills like that. Also, I learned how to use a knife, gun, and my body to protect myself and take down others. Never in a million years would I have thought I would learn to do that.

Thanks to Kat and all the other Keeper trainers, my grief decreased over time. It still made me sad from time to time, but it didn't crush me. I didn't let it. I accepted it and threw myself into training. It was a good distraction. It was so hard, mentally and physically. Some nights I thought I would never make it. I would go back to my room, fall onto my bed, and not get up until the next morning. My brain felt like mush and my body felt like it was falling apart but, after two months of hard training, I had grown. Stronger. Smarter. Capable.

I was ready for my first mission, or that's what the trainers said. I understood how to track people down and how to charm people into answering my questions. I knew how to decode things and pick up fine details others missed. I knew how to defend myself and capture others. They said I was ready, and I tried to believe them. I told myself I wasn't scared in the slightest. But the sweet, sensitive, animal-loving girl inside of me that had been pushed to the side when my parents died was absolutely terrified.

II

Part II: November

13

Lizzie

You know how you can get excited about the first day of school? How you're kind of bored of summer vacation, and you're ready to see your friends, meet new teachers, and just enjoy school again? Like you're not ready for summer to end, but school doesn't seem as bad as it did in May when summer started.

And then a couple weeks go by, and you start to get tired of the whole thing. You have football season and volleyball games, but eventually, those get a little boring too. You start having tests and learning more difficult content. Then a couple months go by, and you just can't wait for Thanksgiving break. The fact that it's coming up is really the only thing getting you through school at this point. Well, it's that time of year.

"Only 20 days left until break," I thought as I got ready for school, after snoozing my alarm twice already. It was a cool, breezy Friday morning, and you could feel Fall in the air, with a hint of the approaching Winter. It was Revere's time to shine. All the trees were red, orange, and brown, and the leaves were falling to the ground and flying through the air like snow.

I put on a cozy, green sweater with my gold necklace and earrings and headed downstairs for breakfast. As I was eating my cereal (Lucky Charms, of course, because they are the best), I got a text from Nolly.

"Hey! Will you pick me up today?" it asked.

"Sure," I replied back.

My friendship with Nolly had been kind of on and off lately. We would hang out at my house after school one day, and then get in a fight and not sit by each other at lunch the next. I knew we were still friends, but it had been rough the past couple of weeks.

Currently, we hadn't spoken in almost a week due to our most recent fight. Nolly had gone to a party with a group of her theater friends, which I totally didn't mind. What I did mind was what happened during and after the party. While she was there, she posted pictures (plural) on her private social media page of her drinking and taking shots. This didn't really surprise me because Nolly had really been getting into that kind of stuff lately. I tried to get her to do less of it and get back to how she was, but I didn't want to be pushy and end up pushing her away.

So anyways, all I did that night was text her and tell her that if she needed me to drive her home I could because, from the pictures, she definitely didn't look sober enough to drive. At around two in the morning, my phone woke me up with a call from Nolly. "Nolly, are you okay?" I asked her when I picked up.

"Heyyyy, Lizzzzie," Nolly slurred. "You wanna come pick me up?"

"I'm on my way," I replied, hanging up.

I got out of bed and headed straight over to the party in

my pink zebra pajama bottoms, leaving a note for my parents hoping they would understand. When I got to the party, Nolly was waiting for me out front. She climbed in, looking totally wasted.

"You okay?" I asked concerned.

"Yeah, it was great. Lotsa boys, lotsa drinking, lotsa dancing. Everything a good party needs," Nolly replied drunkenly. "I thought about callin' you, tryna get you to come, but I knew you wouldn't. You're kinda boring." That stung a little. I knew she was drunk, but still.

"At least I'm not totally wasted," I said.

"You say that like it's a good thing," Nolly replied. "You gotta lighten up. Have some fun every once ina while. Don't be sucha drag."

"Well, this drag is driving you home, making sure you don't get yourself killed in a wreck because you're so drunk," I said, my temper rising.

"I didn't have to call you," Nolly said angrily. "I could have stayed the night with Vicky. She's a good friend." Vicky was the one throwing the party. That stung. We argued back in forth, her calling me a killjoy and telling me to lighten up and me calling her reckless and telling her Vicky can be her new best friend to which she replied, "She already is."

I finally dropped her off at her house, drove home, and cried into my pillow. We hadn't said a word since then until she texted me asking for a ride this morning. That was how our fights usually went. We fought, we didn't talk, then either I apologized, or she would come to me needing something. Then, the cycle repeated. I knew it wasn't healthy, and I honestly wasn't sure how much longer it was going to last.

Anyways, I got up from breakfast, went out to my car, and

headed over to Nolly's house to pick her up because, for the time being, I was still her friend, and I would do almost anything for her. When Nolly got in my car, it was a little awkward at first, but then we started talking like nothing even happened, and I could tell we would be okay. This time at least. I pulled into the parking lot at school, and we headed inside for a long, boring day of class. Only 20 days left.

14

Noah

"Alright, class," said Mr. Bynum, just as the last bell of the day rang. "I expect you to read chapters 5 and 6 of your textbook this weekend. See you on Monday!"

Finally. I did like English class most of the time, but it was my last class of the day, and on Friday afternoons, I had a hard time paying attention to anything other than the clock on the wall above Mr. Bynum's board telling me how much time I had until the weekend. Or until football practice.

It was one of the few weekends we didn't have a football game, so coach insisted we practice. Instead of heading out of the school to enjoy the weekend, I went down the hallway to the locker room. Even though baseball was my main sport, I played football too. A lot of my baseball friends played football in the fall to have something to do since baseball didn't start until the spring. The other reason I played was that I loved the feeling of Friday Night Lights. I loved the feeling of tons of people in the stands screaming. I loved how so many people were involved: the cheerleaders yelling a chant, the band playing a familiar tune, and the dance team doing a pom routine. It was just a fun atmosphere.

After we changed to get ready for what was probably going to be an especially hard practice, the team and I headed out into the cool afternoon to do a series of drills the coach had designed. They were hard, sweaty, and painful. I was definitely going to be sore tomorrow. And I definitely picked up some new bruises from a particularly rough tackle. So, when practice was over, I was relieved. I was tired and sore and very ready to go home.

When we got to the locker room, I got dressed as fast as I could, which was not very fast considering how tired I was. I practically ran out of the locker room and down to my truck. I was so ready to get home and go to sleep on my lumpy living room couch that I didn't see the man in my truck. He was sitting in the driver's seat, but I had gone to the passenger's side to put my backpack and football bag in.

When I opened the passenger door, I saw him and almost shouted out in surprise. Almost, but I didn't. I should have. "Who are you?" I asked instead, starting to get nervous. A man waiting for me in my truck (that I locked this morning) could not be a good thing.

"Get in the truck," he said in a low voice. He was younger looking. Maybe in his early twenties. He had dark hair, but light blue eyes. He had a five o'clock shadow and I could smell the scent of beer and cigarette smoke coming off of him.

It was then that I turned to yell for someone, but the man grabbed my arm before I could. When he did, I looked back at him, and I saw that he was holding a gun. Pointed right at my heart.

"Get. In. The. Truck," he repeated slower, sounding more menacing. I did what he said. What choice did I have? I was freaking out. I was in *my* truck with a stranger who had a gun.

A gun he was not afraid to point at me and probably pull the trigger if I didn't cooperate.

"Good," he said after I had lowered myself into the passenger seat. "Now close the door and hand me your keys and phone." I considered not doing what he said. I know he looked intimidating, but we were in a public place. A school parking lot, nonetheless. Would he really use the gun? But then,

"Do it now or I will not hesitate to use my gun." That answered the question I hadn't even said out loud.

I followed his instructions, handing him my keys and phone. He put my phone in his back pocket, then he put the keys in the ignition, started the truck, and drove away. I felt completely out of control, most likely because I was, and I had no idea what to do. They always tell you to not get in the car with the stranger who has candy, but they never talk about the stranger with the gun. So I just sat there, stealing glances at the stranger every once in a while, trying to not let him catch me looking at him. I tried to make a mental description of him in case I ever needed to fill out a police report. I was trying to think of anything my dad had said to me about his time on the police force that would help me in this situation, but nothing was coming to me.

When we were about 20 minutes away from the school, driving on a road in a wooded area, he pulled off to the side of the road and parked the truck. "Stay here," he growled as he got out of the truck. Again, I thought about going against him, but if I ran, he could shoot me from behind. If I had to guess, he was a pretty good shot, and my running would do me no good. So, I stayed.

The man went around to the side of my truck and grabbed a bag from the backseat. Then, he pulled a blindfold and handcuffs from his bag. He opened up the passenger door and began to cuff and blindfold me. I started to struggle. There was no way I would let him do this. This was too much. Then I felt something cold on my temple. The barrel of the gun. I froze. He finished cuffing and blindfolding me, and that's when the reality of what was happening hit me: I was being kidnapped. And there was nothing I could do about it.

15

Nolly

After school, I had drama club. My absolute favorite part of the day. It beat boring old math classes and stupid English lectures by far. Drama club wasn't really about acting though. I mean, we did a play every year, but I joined because all we really did was gossip. That was why I loved it.

Sure, rehearsing Charlotte's Web or Fiddler on the Roof was great, but talking about why Todd and Jessica broke up? That was the real drama. There were these two other girls, Veronica and Sharone, that I always hung out with.

Veronica had long, silky black hair, rosy cheeks, and bright blue eyes. She was also on the yearbook staff, so she knew about pretty much anything going on in the school. Sharone was tall, had wavy blond hair, and a to-die-for tan. She almost constantly had a boyfriend, so she knew pretty much all the boys in school. Well, at least the ones worth talking about.

When we were supposed to be practicing our lines or designing costumes, we would talk about boys, fashion, and other people's drama, pretty much the best conversation topics of all time. So, when I walked into drama club after school, the first thing I did was find my gossip girls.

"Heeeey!" said Veronica.

"Hey, girl!" I said back.

"So, how was your day? Anything worth noting?" asked Sharone.

"It was fabulous!" I said, even though my day had been kind of gross. From my forgetting my lunch and having to eat the cafeteria's mystery meat to getting a D on my English test, my day had been rough. But no one wanted to hear about that, so I put on my happy face, and we started talking about something juicy Veronica had heard earlier in the day.

"Did you hear that Beth and Marcy got into a fight today?" she asked.

"What?" I said, somewhat shocked. "I thought they were BFFs." They had been, ever since fourth grade. Whenever I thought of one, I thought of the other, and everyone knew if you wanted to invite them to a party, it was both of them or neither. They were a package deal.

"Well, BFFs can break up," Sharone said pointedly at me. I knew we weren't talking about Beth and Marcy anymore. Sharone and Veronica had been trying to get me to say bye to Lizzie and join their friend group for at least a couple of months. I wanted to, but I just hadn't yet. Either I wasn't sure how to ditch her or there was some part of me that didn't want to. Not yet. We'd had so many great times in the past, but lately I had been so fed up with her. Maybe friendships that start in elementary school just aren't meant to last.

"Why don't you just go ahead and ditch her?" Veronica asked bluntly.

"Maybe I will," I said, starting to really think about it. I had fun with these drama club girls, way more fun than I had with

Lizzie, and Lizzie and I just didn't see eye to eye anymore. On anything.

"Good," Sharone said. "Because once you ditch her, you'll probably have way more friends. People will start thinking of you as your own person, instead of just Lizzie's sidekick. And you can finally go to parties without getting in trouble with Lizzie for doing it."

Wow. Did people really think of me as Lizzie's sidekick? I was about to ask Sharone that exact question when the club advisor walked in, and we began to talk about options for the play we would do. I gave suggestions, but my heart was not in it. I was still thinking about Lizzie. Yeah, she was smarter and more involved than I was, and I really only did things at school if she was also doing them . . . Maybe people did really see me as only her sidekick. Her friend who wasn't as good as she was. I was starting to make a name for myself by going to those parties, but Sharone was right. Every time I went, Lizzie would get mad at me.

Should I finally dump her? I thought so. I needed to be my own person and make a name for myself, and I couldn't do that with her holding me back. We were too different, and she was too annoying for me to handle anymore. I began to try to think of how to do it. How to finally be done with her. By the end of drama club, my mind was still occupied, and, to add a cherry on top of my pretty awful day, I missed the bus.

I was standing in the parking lot, wondering what to do, when, out of the blue, a very cute guy came up to me and said, "Hey, did you miss the bus? I can give you a ride home if you want?" Now normally, this would strike me as weird. The little angel on my shoulder would stop me and say (in Lizzie's voice), "He's a stranger! What are you thinking? Why in the world would you take a ride with him?" But, right now, I was done with Lizzie. I wanted to make a name for myself. So, a ride home? With this hot guy? Exactly what I needed.

All thoughts of Lizzie were driven from my mind. "Sure!" I replied, trying not to sound too eager. I followed him over to a small, black pickup truck. He opened the door for me, and I climbed in. We drove for a while and talked about school, family, and other things I couldn't remember because I was distracted by his features. He had blue-black hair that looked as soft as a cloud. His eyes were a steely grey that suggested that he let no one command him. He looked to be around his early twenties, which was probably a little old for me, but I could still admire his features, nonetheless. He had toned muscles that I could see through his shirt, and he had this air of mystery about him that just drew me in.

So, naturally, I didn't notice how long the drive was taking. Nor did I notice that we had passed my neighborhood. And I definitely didn't realize that I had never even given him my address in the first place. In fact, I didn't think anything was out of the ordinary until I saw a sign saying we were leaving the city limits. "Oh . . . um, I think you passed my house." I said a bit nervously, starting to think maybe I had made a bad decision.

"Oh, don't worry," he said. "I know exactly where we are going."

16

Lizzie

Every day after school, I had debate practice. I loved debate. It was like getting to have everyone listen to you talk about your opinion! And I have lots of opinions. I know some people are afraid of public speaking, but not me. I love talking! In front of people, to my friends, and even to myself. I know, I know I'm a weirdo, but talking is definitely my favorite hobby. Unfortunately, you can't really tell people that, hence the reason I do debate.

So, anyways, after school I went to debate practice. We were getting a debate assignment that day, and I was so very excited. I got to the debate room, and the co-sponsors, Mr. and Mrs. Corn, were standing in the front of the room calling names and giving out assignments. The debate sponsors were a married couple, and they were two of the sweetest, selfless, and most fun people I had ever met. They also had two kids who were in high school, Kasen and Kesleigh. Their kids sometimes hung around during debate practice, and when they were there, they would always let us practice our speeches on them. The whole family was just so sweet, and they made debate, one of the best parts of my day, even better.

Anyways, in debate, everyone would get an argument and be assigned what side of the argument they were on. Then, we would have a few weeks to research our argument, and, when the time was up, we would go to a debate tournament and, well, debate.

Needless to say, I was thrilled to be getting an assignment. We had already done one this year, and I had won the tournament. I was hoping to be able to do the same thing again. "Lizzie," Mr. Corn called. I jumped out of my chair and went to the front of the room. "Your argument is about whether social media is harmful or helpful, and you are on the 'Harmful' side," said Mr. Corn.

"Thank you," I said, my mind already turning.

"Go make us another winning argument," he said with a smile.

"Already on it!" I replied, returning to my seat and pulling out my laptop.

Social media wasn't a hard topic, but most people were very opinionated about it, so it would be a challenge to find unbiased sources and points to the argument that hadn't been used yet. I had been in debate all through high school, so Mr. Corn knew I could handle it, but still.

Thankfully, I didn't have too strong of an opinion on the topic, and I could think of points for both sides. It's helpful when you have points for both sides so you can be ready for rebuttal. I powered on my laptop, opened up Google, and began researching. By the end of our hour-long meeting, I had come up with some good ideas for arguments. Nothing too concrete, but definitely a start.

I walked out of school into the brisk autumn day and turned

onto the street towards home. It was the perfect weather outside, and all the leaves on the trees were a beautiful red-orange color. The path I took home cut through some woods and as I entered them, it was like I was in a whole other world, with red, yellow, and orange leaves falling down all around me as I walked. It was just so beautiful and picturesque. I paused and bent down to pick up one of the leaves that had fallen, planning on putting it in my scrapbook.

Then, I heard someone's footsteps coming up behind me. I turned around and saw a guy walking from the direction of the school. "Hey!" he said, still a little way off. I could still see the school, so I thought that maybe he had come from there and just came to tell me I dropped something or left something behind.

"Hi," I said in reply.

"I saw you leave the school, and I noticed you didn't have a ride. Can I drive you home?" the guy asked.

I wasn't exactly comfortable with driving home with a random guy I just met (stranger danger), so I said, "I'm good, thanks." I was perfectly capable of walking myself home, especially on a day as gorgeous as this one.

I turned to go, but he started walking towards me as he said, "No, I insist you let me drive you home." I started backing up. This was getting a little creepy.

"No, no it's fine. I normally walk home, it's not that far," I replied, a little shaken.

He was getting closer to me, and he reached out his arm. I turned away and ran, my fight-or-flight instincts kicking in. Running was really my only option, seeing as how there was no way I could successfully beat up a man twice my size. I mean, what else could I do? There was no way I was riding around in a car with a random creepy guy.

I could hear the man's footsteps behind me. He was chasing after me. I was not very athletic, but he was. He was catching up to me. I threw by backpack at him in an attempt to slow him down, and I flat out sprinted through the woods. The man dodged the bag and began to pick up his pace. My energy was running low. I was slowing down. I tried to run as fast as possible, but he caught up.

He grabbed one of my arms, and, I don't think he expected this, I punched him in the face with the other. It barely made a difference and only made him angrier. I tried to scream for help, but he put his hand over my mouth. He growled and hit me over the head. I collapsed to the ground. He leaned down and grabbed my arms, while I kicked at him. Then, he pinned my legs. He pulled back his fist, and I knew he was going to knock me out. The last thing I saw before he hit me was a malicious gleam in his eyes.

17

Meg

As I headed to the briefing room, I started shaking. The briefing room was the place where we were given our assignments, so I was very, very nervous to be visiting it for the first time. They had told me that I was ready for my first assignment, and I had been trying to convince myself that I was. Taking a deep breath, I tried to calm my nerves, but that didn't help much. I had to stop at the bathroom on the way to throw up.

"It's fine. You're fine. You can do this," I whispered to myself in the bathroom mirror. I had to do this. This was my new life. It had been such a roller coaster the past few months, but if this was my new life, I had better get used to it. I splashed some water on my face, dried myself off, and continued the long walk to the briefing room.

Kat had told me she would be there along with the Director and IM (Individual Missions) Coordinator. The IM was the person who was in charge of everyone's assignments. She and the director would be there to make sure I understood my task and answer any questions I had before I left.

When I arrived in the lobby, the secretary told me to sit and wait. She also gave me a bottle of water and asked if I was all right. I tried to look normal and upbeat and said that I was fine. Apparently, my bathroom pep talk hadn't worked as well as I had hoped. I sat and waited for the debriefing to begin. And waited. And waited. It felt like forever, but it was probably only ten minutes.

I took more deep breaths and tried to build my confidence by thinking about how prepared I was for this. I had spent hours doing practice assignments which meant I had been given old assignments and had to solve them. I had solved every one of them. I had tons of practice in the simulator. The simulator allowed us to face intense and dangerous situations without actually being in any danger. I had escaped a shooter, found my way out of an underground bunker, and evaded a criminal who was following me in a car chase. I was as prepared as possible for whatever mission they would give me. Thinking about that helped me to push all the feelings of fear and doubt away.

Finally, the door to the briefing room opened, and Kat walked out. "You may come in now," she said formally but with a wink, so I knew she was there for me. She really was the best. I walked in and sat down facing Kat, the IM, and the director.

"Welcome, Meg," the director said. "How are you?"

"Good," I managed to get out, trying to sound strong through the sudden burst of anxiety I got when I walked into the room.

"Good," the Director said in turn. "I trust you know why you're here?"

"Yes, Sir," I replied, taking deep breaths. That seemed to be my best strategy for calming down.

"Good. Then I will hand it over to Claudia to explain your first mission."

"Thank you," said Claudia, the IM. "Meg," she began in a serious tone. I could tell Claudia was all business. "The assignment you are being given is very important. Everything I say to you now will be given to you at the end of our meeting in your case file, but it is important that you pay close attention to what I say so you can begin to familiarize yourself with the information. Understand?" I nodded, focused, and she continued.

"A few years ago, there was a man by the name of Bill Smith. Bill was in the business of large-scale forgery. Bill became the closest person ever to completely toppling the United States economy. His counterfeit ring was the largest in the world. He was about to begin printing and distributing money widescale all across the states. He had done it on a small scale before, but his plan all along was to create a counterfeit empire. Thankfully, we caught him the day before his plan would have gone into play. One of his colleges tipped us off and got them all arrested. Even though we tried nearly every means necessary of getting information out of Bill, he would not tell us his plan or any other information about where all his resources were. All we know is that he had a huge printing press capable of making hundreds of thousands of counterfeit dollars per day. Right now, he is locked up in one of the country's most guarded prisons, but his printer is still hidden, and his contacts are still spread across the US."

I nodded along, soaking all this information in. I didn't know why it was all important, only that it was, so I kept listening. "The judge that put Bill behind bars was Judge Kayla Robinson. The police officer that helped capture Bill was Mark Michaels. Both of these people are still alive, and both of them have kids. Here's where we have our problem: both of these people's kids were kidnapped three days ago by none other than Bill Smith's son."

Claudia paused, waiting for me to digest this. It was a lot and I already had lots of questions, but all I could think was that the names of the people whose kids were kidnapped sounded familiar. "Who are the kids?" I asked quietly. "Their names are Lizzie and Noah," Claudia replied.

I was shocked. Beyond shocked. I had thought earlier that I was prepared for anything they threw at me, but I wasn't. Not for this. People I knew, people I had classes with, people I was friends with had been kidnapped? And I was supposed to save them? I'd had classes with Lizzie before and Noah . . . Noah was the closest thing I had ever had to a boyfriend.

Claudia kept going with her story, unaware of the bombshell she had just dropped on me. "We suspect that Bill's son, who he named Cain, wants to get revenge or wants to finish what his father started. Or both. And it's your job to stop him." I stared at her. When she put it like that, it was pretty overwhelming.

"OK," I said in a small voice.

"Your job is to figure out what Cain is up to and put a stop to it. I have full confidence in you. All the information about the kidnapping and Cain's location is in your case file. You are to leave in four hours. You are dismissed."

I got up and slowly walked from the office, in a daze. Kat followed me. When we were in the hallway, Kat started talking. "Oh, my goodness! Your first mission! I'm so excited for you! I am who you report to so call me with questions, concerns, comments, or anything! OK?!"

"OK," I said, still trying to process everything I had just been told. By the time I made it back to my room, Kat had left, and I was slightly calmer. I was worried and I couldn't believe that

I knew the people I was responsible for saving, but that just made it so much more important. I knew these people and I had to give it everything I had to save them.

I read the case file, and it looked like they were all kidnapped after school on Wednesday and taken to . . . somewhere. That was the first step: find out the *Where*. I began to pack my bags and get ready for the trip. I never thought that my first mission, the end of my training, would take me back to where it all started: Home.

18

Nolly

"Who are you," I asked the crazy, but hot, man that appeared to be kidnapping me. While I was starting to completely freak out about the whole driving into the middle of nowhere with a stranger thing, I still couldn't get my brain to stop focusing on how good looking he was. He was definitely too old for me, but I mean, c'mon, the way the sunlight coming in through the windshield glinted off of his dark black hair? I could definitely still appreciate how good he looked.

"A family friend," he replied, answering my question. Since my parents were smugglers and criminals, that wasn't as reassuring as it should have been. "Really?" I asked the guy, trying to get more information from him. "Where are you taking me?"

He replied, but didn't answer my question. "I have your parents' permission to take you. You can call them if you want." So, I did. I pulled out my phone and called my parents. I had to call them twice before they picked up. "Hey," said my dad.

"What do you want?"

"Um, some guy is kidnapping me?" I said like it was a question.

"Oh, yeah. That's right. Go with it. Forgot to tell you. Bye," he said, then hung up. Typical dad, but at least that made it seem like the whole kidnapping thing was approved and I wasn't in any real danger. Hopefully.

"OK," I said to the guy. "What's going on?"

"You're being given the chance of a lifetime," the dude said. I was not expecting that, and I was pretty skeptical. Like this dude could offer me the chance of a lifetime. Yeah, he was good looking, but he didn't look like he had any money or resources. A chance of a lifetime was an offer to act on Broadway or make my own fashion line. I was pretty sure this guy couldn't do either of those things for me.

"To do what?" I asked, confused.

"Follow in your parents' footsteps," he responded.

"Huh?" I said. The footsteps of my smuggler parents?

"Let me explain," the guy said.

"That would be fantastic," I said sarcastically. "It's not like that's what I've been asking you to do for the last ten minutes or anything."

He rolled his eyes at me then said, "I'm Cain. Your parents and my dad are good friends. They worked together on a project a little over fifteen years ago. Their plan failed. Your parents got away. My father was put in prison. Now, I'm going to break my father out and finish what he started all those years ago. But there's another part. Some of the other kids at your school have parents that helped to put my father behind bars. They've been kidnapped as payback. And I'm going to make them do our dirty work, so we won't get caught as easily. You following me?"

I nodded but this was all crazy. I knew my parents were criminals, but I had never heard any details. Also, it was kind of hard to focus on the words Cain was saying when the rest of him just looked so perfect. The sun was starting to go down and his too-old-but-still-gorgeous face was practically glowing in the sunset.

"This is where you come in. You are going to be my inside gal. You will act like you are against me, get them to trust you. And then report to me if they start to make any plans to mess us up. You willing to do that? Your parents said you were. If you aren't willing, then we'll have to hold you hostage until we finish our plan because I've already told you too much information." He paused. Then said, "So? You in?"

Wow. This was it. The moment where I would choose the path of pretty much my whole life. Not to be dramatic or anything. A year ago, I would have said no. But now? I had been feeling so frustrated and bored at school lately. Going to parties and breaking the rules gave me a rush. A rush that I liked. If I did what Cain wanted, I could have that rush all the time. Yeah, I might get caught, but that was part of the thrill. And maybe, if I did this, I would finally get some attention and respect from my parents. I wanted to say yes, but before I said anything, I asked, "Who are the other kids?"

"Their names are Noah and Lizzie," Cain said. It was like he dropped a bomb. Noah? and Lizzie? The boy people ship me with and my used to be best friend? That made the decision harder. But Lizzie wasn't my friend anymore. All she did was correct me and expect way too much from me. Also, I had never really liked Noah in the first place. And the apple doesn't fall very far from the tree; it was time for me to follow in my parents' footsteps.

"I'm in," I said with a smile.

19

Lizzie

When I woke up, I was dazed to say the least. I felt like someone had stuffed a wet towel in my head. What had happened? Where was I? I felt groggy, and I felt like I would pass out again if I moved my head too fast. I looked around, or I tried to. All I could see was black, and I was having trouble breathing. I felt around, but all I could feel was a rough, coarse fabric. I couldn't move my legs. They were tied together. On my head, there was something sticky. Blood. And there was something stuck in it. I pulled it out and realized it was a leaf. A leaf in my hair?

Then I remembered. Being chased. Falling in the leaves. Getting knocked out. This was bad. I wiggled around, trying to figure out my surroundings, when I realized that I was in a sack, like you see in movies. Only real. And it was happening to me. Right now. Not across the theater happening to someone else on a big screen while I'm safely watching with a bucket of popcorn and a package of milk duds.

All of a sudden, I felt claustrophobic. The sack was getting smaller and smaller, and breathing was getting harder and harder. I was starting to full on panic. I screamed, terrified I would die in the dark sack. Suddenly, something hard hit my head. "For the fifth time! Shush!" A man's voice. The kidnapper.

Wait, the fifth time? Had this already happened and I just couldn't remember? This just kept getting worse. I had no idea where I was and no idea how long I had been knocked out. Where was I? What if I never saw my family again? How was I going to escape? I had to get out of here.

I quieted the thoughts in my head, so I could listen to my surroundings. I knew I was in a car because I could feel the movement and hear the engine. I heard the quiet hum of the tires on the road, the gentle, but slightly ragged, breathing of the man, the sound of a train in the distance, the sound of a turn signal blinking then the feel of the car turning. I stayed still like that for around an hour listening. For what? Who knows? Maybe I was just trying to stay alert and not lose my sanity. Maybe it made me feel like I was doing something productive that would help me escape.

Finally, after what felt like an eternity, the car stopped. The kidnapper got out of the car, then came to get me. He picked me up, or should I say he picked up the bag with me in it and carried me through a door and down a ladder. I was still blindfolded and was completely disoriented. Once we got wherever we were going, he closed a door behind him and opened the bag. He pulled me out and I felt myself being cuffed to a wall. Then, he pulled the blindfold off.

It was so bright I had to close my eyes again. Once my eyes adjusted, I saw that the room I was in was more of a cell. Each of the four cement walls had a pair of handcuffs attached to them. There was a small window near the ceiling with thick metal bars. The floor was also cement and it had a drain in the middle. It was definitely not a comforting sight. The kidnapper was about 5'9" with long brown hair pulled into a low, greasy ponytail. He was clean shaven but had a unibrow. Before I could analyze him anymore, He turned and walked out of the room. And locked the door behind him.

20

Noah

Sitting in the passenger seat of my truck blindfolded, cuffed, and kidnapped was the most terrifying thing that ever happened to me. I was scared. I was confused. This man had a gun that he had pointed at me. Me! I was a quiet kid. A good kid. I played sports. I volunteered at the children's hospital. I was normal. But now, for some reason, I was being kidnapped. Never in a million years would I have thought I would say those words.

We drove for around an hour, then pulled over. How long would it be until someone noticed I was missing? My dad worked a late shift tonight. He wouldn't be home until at least 10:30. What would he do when he realized I wasn't home?

"Get out," the man said, "but don't run." I felt cold metal against my face. His gun. He was making sure I knew he was still in charge. I got out of the truck and stood still, unable to see anything because of my blindfold. I tried wiggling my face to get it to move. Eventually, with a lot of raised and lowered eyebrows and some nose-wiggling, the blindfold slipped enough for me to be able to see a little bit.

We were in the middle of nowhere. All I could see was trees. The road stretched out to my right and left but eventually just disappeared into more trees. Was the kidnapper going to leave me on the side of the road? Was he just taking my truck? I loved my truck, but I'd rather her be kidnapped then me. Just as my hopes began to rise, they crashed down again because the kidnapper grabbed me by the arm and started walking me somewhere.

We walked a little way before I got fed up. This was stupid. I had no idea what he was going to do with me, but chances are, if he hadn't killed me or abandoned me yet, he needed me for something. For what? No clue, but I convinced myself he wasn't going to shoot me. I decided to fight back. I wouldn't go without a struggle. I was still handcuffed, but I pulled back my shoulder and rammed it into the guy's chest. He groaned a little, then reacted fast. I was still mostly blind folded, but I could feel what he did. He pulled out a knife and ran it down my arm, creating a deep cut. I cried out in pain. "Don't you ever do anything like that again," the man growled. "Because there's more where that came from."

Before I could think about what he said, he grabbed me by the other arm and fixed my blindfold more securely over my eyes. He pulled me through what I assumed was more forest, but I couldn't see, and I was distracted by my arm, which felt like it was on fire. I could feel the blood running down my arm and dripping off. This was so frustrating. There was nothing I could do. I had tried fighting, but all that got me was an injury and a threat. *There's more where that came from.* Did he have another weapon? Or was he going to use his knife again if I did something he didn't like? Or use his gun? I was still pretty sure he wouldn't kill me, but with my blood still trickling down my arm, that thought wasn't as reassuring as it was a few minutes ago. I guess I was just going to have to wait to see where the kidnapper took me and come up with a plan from there. Either way, I was going to get out of this mess.

Eventually, we got to another car that the man shoved me into. I didn't move for the rest of the trip. When the car stopped, the kidnapper pulled me out and took me inside a building, through a door, and down a ladder. That was all I could figure out from behind the blindfold. He cuffed me to a wall and took my blindfold off. Then he left. I looked around and saw that I was in a cement room . . . with another person who was also chained up. A girl. A girl that looked awfully familiar.

21

Nolly

When we got to Cain's little hide out, I was a little . . . how do I put this? Grossed out? Concerned? The "hide out" looked to be more of a huge run-down shack buried deep in the forest. Cain's credibility was dropping rapidly. "Um, what is this?" I asked him, gesturing to the decrepit building behind me.

"Don't worry," he said with a smirk. "It only looks like this on the outside to keep people away." *He better be telling the truth,* I thought. Because otherwise this whole deal was off. I was not about to live in a shack.

I climbed out of the car and headed towards what looked like the entrance. Cain followed behind me and pulled out a key to unlock the door. "You keep this door locked?" I asked. "Because it looks like a strong gust of wind could knock it down. I feel like a lock is pretty pointless." Cain glared at me, and I took that as my cue to shut up. He unlocked the door, and we stepped across the threshold into an empty room filled with nothing but cobwebs and dust. "Um, is this all there is?" I

86

asked. "Am I being pranked right now?"

"Would you just shut up for one second so we could actually get to the hide out?" Cain said angrily.

"Okay, okay, calm down," I said. Cain walked to the corner of the room and bent down to mess with something on the floor. My curiosity was piqued, so I went over to where he was and saw a trap door! That made so much more sense. The real hide out would be under there.

Cain unlocked and opened the trap door and gestured for me to go down first. I climbed down a ladder and into a well-lit room. It had a couch in front of a small table and a TV. Across from that there was a small kitchen with a fridge, microwave, and oven. There were also two hallways branching off from the main room. Not exactly luxurious, but much better than the shack.

"OK," Cain said after climbing down the ladder behind me. "This is the main room. Down that hall is the cell and down the other one is mine and the other guys' rooms and my office."

"Other guys?" I asked. I didn't know we weren't working alone. "Yeah, I've got two other guys working with me. That a problem?"

"Nope, not at all," I said, while thinking the exact opposite.

I didn't want to work with other people. I wanted to complete the job with only Cain and me. I wanted to prove to my parents I could do what they did and that wasn't going to happen if two other random dudes were here taking all the good jobs. I'd never really been good at sharing the spotlight, and that wasn't going to start now.

"OK, Nolly," Cain said, startling me out of my thoughts. "I'm going to cuff and blindfold you now and take you to the room with the other prisoners. It's all just for show, so they think you were really kidnapped like them. Ready?"

"Of course!" I sang, forgetting my worries and getting excited for my debut. My debut in crime (after this I was actually involved; there would be no going back), but also a debut in acting of sorts. It would take a great deal of my acting skills to pull this off. Thankfully, I was the best actress I knew.

Once I was cuffed and blindfolded, Cain led me through some doors and cuffed me to the wall in the prison room. Then, Cain removed my blindfold and left, and I looked around at my fellow prisoners. Putting on a petrified face I whispered, "Do you guys know what's going on?" My voice shook. Man, I was good at this. No one responded. They had no idea what they were in for.

22

Meg

When I arrived back in Revere, I checked into my hotel. I had driven past this hotel so many times, but I never would have thought I would be staying in it. I always figured if I came back here, I would just stay with my parents. My parents . . . "Shake it off, Meg," I said to myself. "Stay focused."

My code name for this assignment was Rebeca Stewart. Rebeca Stewart didn't worry about the past, she focused on her case. I got my hotel key and headed up to my room. Once I had unpacked, I began working on the case right away. The local police had already begun to investigate, so I decided to head over to the station to see what work they had done. Kat had told me that she had called ahead to the police station and told them that I was coming. She didn't give them all the information, only that a young agent by the name of Rebeca Stewart would be asking about the case. I was a little skeptical about just walking into the police station and asking for evidence to a kidnapping that was making national news, but that's what I did. Thankfully, I had a badge with Rebeca's name on it that made me look official, so if they wouldn't help me right away, I had that back up.

I got to the station and went to the secretary's desk. "Hello," she said in a cheery voice. "How may I help you?"

"I'm Rebeca Stewart, and I'd like to speak to the chief, please, about the kidnappings. I'm with Kathleen." It was like I flipped a switch; the secretary was all business now.

She stood up, told me to follow her and walked briskly down a bare white hallway. I followed her, and then we went through a door marked "Investigation."

"This is Rebeca Stewart," the receptionist said, then turned around and left. All eyes were on me. I was surprised at how easy this had been so far. Kat and the agency must have more influence than I thought. Either way, it was my time to shine.

The chief stood up and held out his hand. "Hello, Rebeca. Nice to meet you."

"Likewise," I said. Now that the pleasantries were exchanged, we started to work. The police that were on the case, which was most of the station because it was a very small town, showed me all the evidence they had collected.

First, they showed me Noah's file. They told me that they believed that Noah got out of school first. They had statements from other football players saying that they saw Noah leave the field in a hurry. No one saw him get in his truck or leave. They found his truck a couple of miles east of the town, which clearly suggested that whoever kidnapped him had headed east. They inspected the truck for fingerprints but found none. The only thing they found in the truck was a knife with blood on it. They had been able to confirm that it was Noah's. I had learned in training that I have to separate my feelings from every investigation that I did. It was so hard to do at that moment. I was trying so hard to not think the worst. Noah, my used-to-be-almost-boyfriend, was fine. He had to be.

Noah's situation was taking us nowhere, so we moved onto Lizzie. Her debate practice got out 30 minutes after Noah's practice, so it sounded like there might have been more than one kidnapper. They had statements from Lizzie's classmates saying they saw her start her normal walking home route. There were also some statements saying they saw a tall, dark haired man follow Lizzie. A few blocks up, Lizzie's backpack was found, laying on the ground. Further ahead, there were signs of struggle and a smear of Lizzie's blood on the ground. "So much blood," I thought, fearfully. "No, they're fine," I told myself. I had to stay strong if I wanted to save them.

After the police had shown me their clues, we shared a glum expression. Our clues showed that there were probably two kidnappers, they headed east, and they were violent. Not much to work with at all. And we had to find them before the situation got worse. We were miles behind them already.

23

Lizzie

I looked around the small cement room at the other captives. One of them had soft blond hair, blue eyes and built muscles. His shirt was sweaty, and he had a long cut down his arm that didn't help to ease my fears. He looked frustrated, but not really fearful. The other person in the prison was . . . Nolly?!?! She had just been cuffed to the wall, and I hadn't realized it was her. She didn't look the worse for wear (no huge cuts or nasty bruises or anything), but I could hardly believe it was her. I was both not happy and happy to see her there.

Of course, I didn't want her to be in this awful situation and I would never want her to be hurt but at the same time I was thankful I had a friend to lean on during this mess. I tried to smile at her and reassure her or something, but she was staring intently at a corner of the ceiling with a scared, far-off look in her eyes. I felt so bad for her. She looked like she might be in shock.

I turned my attention back to the boy. He looked familiar. I was pretty sure he also went to our school, but he was a grade older. I was still trying to remember more about this boy, mainly to distract myself from what was going on when he spoke up. "Hey," he whispered. "I'm Noah. I feel like I've seen you around, but what is your name? You look familiar."

"I'm Lizzie. I think we had geometry together last year," I replied, finally realizing where I knew him from. "Oh, that's right," Noah said. "Mr. Charles was the best."

Noah and I rambled on about Mr. Charles' class for probably 20 minutes, desperately trying to find something familiar in this situation. I think we were both trying to distract ourselves from all the whys and what-ifs. Why us? Why were we the ones kidnapped? What if we didn't make it home? What if no one ever found us?

Eventually, Noah and I covered everything we could talk about related to Mr. Charles and geometry, and the room grew quiet. Questions started to fill my head. What was going to happen to us? We had been sitting there for what felt like forever. I needed someone to tell me what was going on. I glanced over at Nolly, who still hadn't said anything. She was still staring at that spot on the ceiling, and it looked to me like she was shaking.

"Hey, Nolly, are you alright?" I asked her, knowing that was a dumb question. I mean clearly none of us were alright, we had been kidnapped for Pete's sake, but I was hoping the question would comfort her or at the very least shake her from her trance. "I'm scared, Lizzie," Nolly whispered, locking her eyes onto mine.

"So am I," I said, my voice shaking a little. "But . . ." There had to be a "but." There had to be a way for us to get out of here. There had to be some sort of bright side or silver lining to focus on, even though we were chained to a wall and locked away in a prison cell. There had to be a positive outlook, but I couldn't think of one.

"But we are going to come up with a plan to get out of here," said another voice. Noah's. "We have to."

24

Noah

We sat in that room for a long time. There were no clocks or windows or anything that would give us a sense of the time. Occasionally, we would whisper about random things just to keep ourselves sane. I knew we were all scared. Who wouldn't be? But for me personally, I was more angry than afraid. I didn't really know why. I think I was mad that they thought they could just take us away from our families and friends and entire lives and get away with it. I was mad that they expected us to just go along with it, so I wasn't going to! I was going to fight back as much as possible and do everything I could to get myself, Lizzie, and Nolly out of here. I was not just going to sit around and wait for someone to rescue us, and I definitely was not going to go along with whatever the kidnappers wanted.

What was it that they wanted? I wondered. Was it a ransom? My dad and I had a decent house and we both had trucks to drive, but we were not rich by any means. I didn't know about the girls, but I figured a ransom was not what the kidnappers wanted. Why else would they kidnap us? Was there something they wanted us to do? If so, why us? To my knowledge, the three of us didn't share any special skills or anything. What did we have in common? Were we picked on purpose or was it random? I was going to go crazy from all the questions that didn't have answers, the biggest one being how were we going to escape? I tried to come up with a plan, but my mind was blank. I had next to no information to work with, so I couldn't make any plans. Yet.

I looked around the room at the two girls. I'd had a few classes with Lizzie, and she was pretty well known around school. She was involved in things, and I think I remember her leading some cheers in the student section at football games. I knew who she was, but I didn't really know her. Nolly on the other hand . . . I knew plenty about Nolly. I had started off the school year liking her, but she had kind of gone off the deep end recently. I had heard from some friends that she spent almost every weekend partying, and every weekend she had a different guy. She was still absolutely gorgeous, even now in this prison cell, but looks aren't all that matters in a girl. She used to be kind, funny, and spontaneous. She was over dramatic, but in a fun way. Now? It seemed like she was desperate for attention, so desperate she was willing to hang out with any guy who would give it to her. I felt bad for her, but I didn't think this new version of her was a girl I wanted to be with.

She looked so scared, though, shaking against the wall she was chained to. Lizzie looked like she was holding up well, but not Nolly. The room was small enough and we were close enough that I figured I could reach her. The chains attached to the handcuffs allowed just enough movement. I went to try to pat her on the back, but a shot of pain went through my arm. My arm was still bleeding from the knife, and anytime I moved it, white hot pain shot through it. I tried not to think about what the man meant when he said, "There's more where that came from."

But again, those words really made me more angry than fearful. How terrible do you have to be to kidnap a kid, drag a knife through their arm, and then threaten them? Those are the people my dad worked so hard to put behind bars. My dad. I had been trying to avoid thinking of him because I preferred to be angry, but when I thought of him the fear and sadness started to creep in.

What if I never got to see him again? He was all I had, and I hadn't even gotten to see him that morning because he had to go on patrol early to cover for another officer. What had he done when he realized I hadn't come home? Was he working on the case, trying to bring us home? I quickly snapped out of my thoughts though, when the door opened and three men, one of them being my kidnapper, walked in. I got a glimpse of a long hallway with a couch and TV at the end. Where were we? Then they closed and locked the door behind them.

25

Nolly

I'm an amazing actor. I totally had them fooled. Lizzie was all like "Are you okay?" and Noah kept glancing at me sympathetically. I pretended to stare off into space, like I was in some sort of petrified trance, and it worked like a charm. I was absolutely killing this role. Unfortunately, I was starting to get kind of bored because we had been in that room literally forever.

Finally, I heard footsteps in the hall. When Cain and his cronies walked in, I let out a little yelp and scooted back. Like I said, absolutely killing it. Cain laughed a cruel, heartless laugh. He knew I had everyone fooled. "Hello," Cain said. "I guess you are curious about why you are here." He said it like he was at a business meeting, not talking to three prisoners in a cement cell. Well, two prisoners and an adorable undercover spy.

I glanced over at Lizzie and could tell she was angry and annoyed. She'd been scared up till now, but I think her spunk and frustration had blocked out her fear for a second. She had an expression on her face that she normally had right before she let someone have a piece of her mind. "Oh, yes!" Lizzie exploded.

"We are just *slightly* curious about why we were beaten up and kidnapped. Just wondering a *little* about why we have been kept in this cement room for so long and who in the world you people are. This all generally happens on a regular basis, so we are only a *little* curious about what's going on!"

Lizzie looked outraged, then I think she realized what she had just said. A look of terror crossed her face. "Sorry. Please don't hurt me," she squeaked out. She was still out of breath from her speech and looked pretty terrified, but Cain wasn't the least bit rattled. He walked up to her and glared. The fear melted off her face, and she glared right back. Then, without warning, he slapped her in the face so hard she was knocked over. I gasped and covered my face (more fabulous acting but also a little bit of real shock), and Noah freaked out.

"You can't just hit her like that!" he yelled, pulling at his handcuffs from across the room. "You awful, horrible, terrible-" *Thud.* Cain had pulled a throwing knife out of his coat pocket and threw it. It landed right next to Noah, pinning his shirt to the wall, effectively cutting off the rest of what he was going to say.

Cain's crony #1 walked over to Noah and pulled the knife out. "Got anything else to say?" the man asked. Noah just glared at him. If looks could kill . . .

"Alright," Cain said. "Now that we have gotten acquainted with each other, I will tell you why you are here." He then went on to explain what I already knew about Lizzie and Noah's parents, his dad, and how they would be doing the dirty work. Noah glared at him the whole time, and Lizzie alternated between staring down at her feet and shooting angry looks at Cain and his cronies.

I turned my attention back to Cain's monologue as he started to explain the plan. "The first part of my plan is breaking my father out of prison. Tomorrow, you kids and Huxley here (he pointed to crony #1) will go to the prison in Boston, visit my father and get information about him. I can't go for obvious reasons, but you should have no trouble getting in to see him. Huxley is listed as his nephew. Then, I will create a plan to break my father out of prison based on intel you gather. That's as much of the plan I'm going to tell you, for obvious reasons. Now you all should get some sleep. You'll leave for the prison at 6 AM, which is only six hours away. Oh, and, by the way, don't even think about disobeying me because if you do, I will not hesitate to dispose of you and make it look like an accident, if you get what I mean."

I gasped and covered my mouth. Had to keep up appearances, but also, that would be really violent. "You're alive now because I need you to do a few things for me, but those things can just as easily be done by two people," Cain finished. With that, he turned and left. Man was I glad to be on his side.

26

Meg

Since there were no leads at the police station, I went to the only other place in the area that may have clues: the prison. I was hoping to be able to talk to Cain's father and get some sort of information out of him. It was a stretch, but I really didn't have any other ideas. Cain's father was being held in the federal prison in the Massachusetts capital, Boston, which was only about a half an hour away, so that's where I headed.

The drive over was beautiful. I drove through a forest of trees with red, orange, and yellow leaves. They were falling and swirling around, but, as much as I wanted to, I couldn't focus on the beauty around me. I was completely sucked into the case and focused on everything that was at stake. If I messed up, people I knew could end up dead. I was trying to pretend to myself that I didn't know the people who were kidnapped, but I was epically failing.

Whenever I thought about Lizzie, I remembered all the classes we had shared and the projects we had worked on together. Even though she was a grade younger than I was,

I had kind of looked up to her. She was an overachiever, so we'd had quite a few classes together and she always excelled in them. She was also so involved in the school, always participating in the pep rallies and student section. I didn't know her that well, but almost everyone in the school knew she was kind and full of spirit, which I admired.

And I didn't even want to try and to figure out my feelings about Noah. I was so scared when I found out he was one of the kids kidnapped, and I think it's because, even though we hadn't really hung out recently, he still meant a lot to me. Maybe those feelings from freshman year never really went away; they were just pushed down. When I thought about losing him, it struck a chord deep inside me. I didn't want to live in a world without Noah, and I was surprised that my feelings about him were so strong.

Eventually, I pulled up to the large grey building with the words UNITED STATES FEDERAL PRISON on the front in big bold letters. The parking lot was empty except for a white car that was pulling away, so I parked right next to the entrance. I got out of my own small car and walked into the prison. There were some old chairs grouped together next to a desk in the middle of an open room, and there were guards standing in front of both sides of a heavy, black door at the back of the room. I walked up to the guard sitting at the desk.

"Hello, Sir," I said. "What is the protocol for visiting inmates here?" I wasn't even sure I would be able to visit Bill since he was such a high-profile criminal. I was probably going to need my badge for this one, but even then, I wasn't sure.

"Which inmate would you like to visit?" the guard asked.

"Bill Smith," I replied.

"Wow, that inmate is popular today," the guard said under

his breath.

He was popular? Did that mean someone else had visited him? I had a hunch. "What do you mean by that?" I asked the guard, hoping my hunch was right.

"Um, I'm sorry, Ma'am," the guard replied. "I can't discuss a prisoner's visiting history."

I pulled out my badge and handed it to him. He glanced at it, then back up at me.

"Well, in that case," he said, handing back my badge, "three kids came in just a few minutes ago asking about Bill. Unfortunately, I had to tell them the same news I'm about to tell you. Bill is dead. Died in his sleep last night."

"He's dead?" I blurted out, shocked. The guard nodded somberly.

"It's a real shame too," he said. "Bill hadn't gotten any visitors the whole time he's been here, and the day after he dies, he gets two different groups."

The kids that visited him had to be Lizzie, Nolly, and Noah, right? And they were probably with Cain or someone Cain sent in his place. I mean what other kids would ask about Smith?

"When did Bill's other visitors come in?" I asked the guard.

"Oh, they left right before you got here," the guard said. Maybe they were in that white convertible I saw on my way in!

"Do you happen to have the security tape for the parking lot?" I asked the guard, deciding to follow my hunch all the way through. I could be on to something. He began to look uncomfortable. "I don't think I have the clearance to give you that. Maybe you should talk to my boss about this. You want me to show you to her office?"

"Yes, please," I replied, getting antsy. I was ready to know if my hunch was right. I didn't know what I was going to do if the guard's boss refused to show me the security videos. We arrived at her office and the guard knocked on the door.

"Come in," a voice said. The guard opened the door and introduced me. "This is Rebeca Stewart. She's on official business and would like to see some security tapes." With that, he turned around and left. The boss, who was short and had light blond hair pulled back into a tight bun, stood up to shake my hand.

"I'm Abigail Sanders, nice to meet you," she said.

"Likewise," I replied, handing her my badge. She examined it, and my heart was racing.

"Looks like this checks out," she said. "What tapes are you needing?" I breathed a sigh of relief and explained that I needed the tapes from the parking lot and lobby from the past few hours.

"Alright then. Follow me and I'll get you a copy of that tape," she said. We went down a hallway, through a small white door, and into a dark room filled with video monitors.

As the boss typed on the computer to get a copy of the tape for me, I thought about my course of action. If I could get a look at who got into the white car, I would be able to tell for sure if it was Lizzie, Nolly, and Noah. It was a bit of a stretch and it seemed a little too good to be true, but I had to try. I had to follow my gut.

It would be even better if I could see the license plate number and get a good look at the person in the car who was driving. That would mean that I may have a shot at finding these people.

Abigail handed me a flash drive with a recording of the parking lot and lobby over the last five hours. I thanked her then asked if I could see Bill's cell. She called up the guard from earlier to take me to see it, wishing me luck as she went back to her office. The guard then took me through a series of hallways to get to Bill's cell. I looked around in hopes that there would be something helpful, but the cell was bare. Unfortunate, but not surprising. I said thanks to the guard, then went to watch the tape in my car. It was time to find out for sure who was in that white convertible.

27

Lizzie

"Rise and shineeee," someone sang in a deep, gravelly voice, waking me up. It was still dark. Why was I getting up? Was it time for school? Then my eyes adjusted. Oh right. The cell. The kidnappers. All that fun stuff.

"Here's something to eat. Wake up and eat it quick. We leave for the jail in 10 minutes," the creepy guy that kidnapped me said, placing a bowl of something in front of me. Oatmeal? Cereal? I really couldn't tell, but I ate it anyway because I was starving. They hadn't given us dinner last night. I saw Nolly and Noah also gulping down their breakfasts. They had to be just as hungry as I was. In no time, we had finished eating and Cain and both of the other creepy guys were back in the cell, telling us it was time to go.

"This is how it's going to work," Cain explained. "You three will go into the jail and ask to visit Bill Smith. They should let you in. Today is visiting day. When you get in to see Bill, you will ask him these questions," he said, handing Nolly a list. "And write down the answers. Make sure you are absolutely clear on the instruction on how to access the bunker and continue his work."

A bunker? His work? Apparently, that was all the information we were going to get. "Huxley, here, is going to drive you, but he will wait in the car. If you try to pull anything clever, he is armed and is not afraid to shoot you." Wow. Way to be blunt. "Are we clear?" Cain asked, making eye contact with each of us. We all nodded. Cain then made us all wear wigs and dress up to go to the prison. They blindfolded us and led us back out of the building. Then, they helped us into the car, and we took off.

We went with the guy that kidnapped me and drove over to the prison in a white convertible I hadn't seen before. Where did they get all these cars? When we got there, a guard told us that Cain's dad had died the night before. Uh, oh. This threw a major wrench into Cain's plans, which was a good and bad thing for me, Nolly, and Noah. Good because it meant Cain's plan was messed up, even if only temporarily. Bad because my kidnapper friend looked like he might explode from anger when we told him, and I was worried we may face some sort of repercussions for this problem, even though we really had nothing to do with it.

After we explained what the guard had said to us, he told us to get in the car, and we took off just as a small navy car pulled up. I thought nothing of it, but Noah was straining to see it. The kidnapper was on his phone pulling up Cain's contact info when Noah whispered to me, "Did you see who got out of that car? It was Megan Martin!" Meg! What a coincidence that we would see someone from school visiting the jail that we happened to be at. Was it really a coincidence? And it wasn't just someone from school. It was someone that used to go to our school but had disappeared a few months ago. Then, for some reason, a conversation I had heard popped back into my head: that kid who said maybe Meg went to the government to work as a spy.

I leaned over and whispered to Noah, "Do you know what happened to her? Why she disappeared?" He shook his head no. I told him the conversation I had overheard.

"I mean, it's possible," he said dubiously. "Not probable though."

"I know," I whispered back with a sigh. "I think I'm just trying to find something, some type of hope, to cling to at this point." He nodded and we went back to our own thoughts. I knew there was no way Meg was a spy, only wishful thinking, but, either way, I just hoped someone was out there looking for us.

28

Noah

We drove away from the jail for a little while, then pulled over on the side of the road. "Stay here," Huxley said, getting out of the car. Thankfully, he hadn't put our blindfolds on when we got back in the car, so I could see Huxley through the front windshield. He was on the phone, probably with Cain, and their conversation looked pretty intense.

Normally, I would be trying to read his lips and figure out any details that might help us get out of here, but I was distracted. I kept thinking about the girl I had seen at the prison. She had a different hair color than Meg, but her eyes looked the exact same. The same beautiful blue color that looked like the line between the sky and the ocean. And, if she was working for the government like Lizzie said, a hair change would make sense. It was definitely her.

I hadn't seen her since the day she left. I had thought about her every once in a while, about how if she hadn't left, we might have been able to be friends again. I had even tried to find her on social media. I had messaged her a few times, but she never responded. I had asked around, but no one knew why she had left, and no one had seen her since then. Everyone talked about it for a while, the girl who had disappeared, but eventually, that became old news.

I tried to remember the day she left. I had seen her in the hallway, and I had noticed that she looked worried. Later that day in one of my other classes, the teacher was calling roll, and when she got to Meg's name, there was no response. Over the next few days, I began to hear the rumors that she had disappeared. I had started to worry about her. Even though we hadn't talked in a while, she was such an important part of my life freshman year, and I was starting to realize there was a part of me that still cared about her. A lot.

I had decided to ask my dad about the whole thing, thinking if she really was missing, there would be an investigation going on at the station. He had told me that there were no active missing children cases, but there was a car wreck earlier in the week. Both people in the wreck had died and they had her same last name. I assumed that the people that died must have been Meg's parents, which would help to explain the disappearance. But where she went? I still didn't know. Lizzie's theory about her being a spy could be an answer, but I thought it was pretty far-fetched. We were probably just being desperate, hoping there was someone out there looking for us. That had to be it. I knew that I had never heard of a secret government organization that used kids before. I guess that was the point of it being secret, but getting kids whose parents had just died to work for the government? Seemed kind-of cruel to me.

After a long, drawn-out conversation on the phone, Huxley finally got back in the car. "Where are we off to now?" Lizzie asked.

Huxley glared at her, then said, "To the law office." The law office? Why there? At this point though, I was used to having thousands of questions and zero answers. We drove to the office, then Huxley explained.

"Cain called Bill's lawyer and told him I was coming. Cain told the lawyer to let me see the will, so I'm going to go in, take a few pictures, then come right back. You three are staying in the car because I don't want you to come inside if you don't have to. I'm locking the car, so you're stuck here. Got it?" We all nodded, and Huxley got out of the car and went inside.

As soon as he was out of sight, I unbuckled my seatbelt. "C'mon guys," I said. "Let's try to break the windows and get out of here."

"Alright, what do you think is the best way to do it?" Lizzie asked, ready to go.

Nolly, on the other hand, looked scared. "Um, we shouldn't do that," she said.

"Why not?" I shot back, fired up. "This might be our best chance to escape."

"Huxley said to stay put though and he sounded really serious," Nolly replied. "He probably has a gun on him."

"So what?" I asked. "He can't shoot us from inside the building."

"True but . . ." Nolly seemed to be grasping at straws, trying to find reasons why we shouldn't try to escape. Why was she so determined to stay in the car?

"If we break the window, won't the car alarm go off?" she asked. That made me pause. Would it? I didn't know how sensitive the alarms on this car were. It would make sense for them to have a high sensitivity though. While I was debating in my head whether we should go through with it or not, Lizzie interrupted my train of thought.

"It doesn't matter anyway," she said. "He's on his way back." Glancing out the front window, I saw Huxley walking back toward the car. Shooting a glare in Nolly's direction, I buckled my seatbelt and waited for Huxley to reach the car, angry that we missed our chance.

After we got back to the base, which I could now see looked like a small, abandoned shack, they brought us back to our cell and cuffed us up. As I was trying to get into a comfortable position with my hands cuffed to a wall, the mysterious Cain walked into the room. It's like the very air froze when he came in.

"So, turns out your trip to town wasn't a total waste after all," he said. He didn't sound the least bit upset about his father being dead, which only added to his cold demeanor. "The will that was left contains a secret code with information on a scavenger hunt of sorts that ends in a place with all the equipment my father used to run his, shall we say, business. I believe he put it in scavenger hunt form so that it would be difficult to find and not fall into the wrong hands. So, tomorrow we leave this place to follow the scavenger hunt clues. They'll bring in dinner shortly."

And he left. What the heck? This was wild. A scavenger hunt to find equipment to start up a criminal business? As I was trying to wrap my head around everything Cain just said, the other one of Cain's men (Harrison I think was his name) brought our dinner. "Dinner" turned out to be a bowl of brown goop with red chunks in it. But we were hungry enough to eat it.

After they took our dinner dishes, I went back to thinking about Meg. I decided that I needed to get my hands on that will.

And maybe even find a way to get it to someone, anyone, who might be able to help us. I was willing to try anything to get out of here, even if it was a really long shot.

29

Nolly

That night, once everyone else was asleep, one of Cain's cronies came to get me. I followed him out of the cell and into the main room. From there, we went down the other hallway and through a door into what looked like an office.

Cain was sitting in a leather chair at a wood desk in an otherwise empty room. His grey eyes looked stormy, and his hair fell in waves across his eyes. His face was partly in shadow because of the dimly lit room, so I couldn't make out his expression. In this lighting and in the bare room, he looked absolutely terrifying, like some villain in a movie. I guess he kind of was, but I wasn't going to let him intimidate me. He needed me. I was absolutely vital to this operation, and I knew it, so I walked across the room and sat down on the edge of the desk.

Cain looked at me, studied me. Then, with a smirk he said, "Hello, Nolly."

"Hello," I replied smoothly.

"Any news for me?" he asked.

"Not really," I responded. "They almost tried escaping today in the parking lot at the law office, but I stopped them." I was proud to tell Cain about my accomplishment today. I will admit, I was worried because I had no idea if the car alarm would actually go off, but if it came down to it, I was prepared to blow my cover and make sure they stayed in the car no matter what.

"What was their plan?" Cain asked.

"They were going to break the car windows, but I tried to stall them, then I told them it would probably trigger the car alarm."

"Ahh, I see," Cain replied. I thought he would be angry, and while I could see that there definitely was some anger, his expression mainly looked thoughtful.

"Well, good job then, Nolly."

"Thank you," I said with a smile. I was not really expecting praise, and I felt like I was practically glowing because of it. "Will you tell me the plan now?" I asked him. I knew he didn't have to, but I was testing him, to see if he really trusted me. Now that he saw what I could do and how important I was to his mission, he really had no reason to not trust me.

"Well, aren't you fiery?" he started with a smirk. "Tomorrow we are going to the first place in the will. It's . . ."

"Wait," I interrupted him. "What exactly was in the will. Explain how this works."

"Okay, okay, calm down. My father left me the will and he encoded it with information on how to restart his business. Apparently, instructions to get to my father's hidden bunker were spread out and hidden in a scavenger hunt type puzzle. Each city mentioned in the will is where we are supposed to go and there are different instructions to the bunker in each city."

"What's in the bunker?" I asked, curious about the whole purpose behind our operation. Cain paused. I could tell he was considering whether to tell me or not.

"A printing press," he finally replied, "for printing counterfeit money. Along with probably hundreds of thousands of dollars already printed." That was not what I expected. But I knew what it meant. We would be very, very rich if we could pull this off.

"Anyway," Cain said. "I have something for you." He pulled out a disk with a bunch of different words and letters on it and set it on the desk.

"Thanks," I said skeptically, not sure what it was. "Um, what is it?"

"It's a decoder for the will. The will is encoded with a very, very difficult code to break. My dad and I used it all the time growing up and the two of us are the only ones that know how to break it. I mailed your parents a copy of the will earlier today, and now I'm giving you the decoder. That way in case I get caught, someone will be able to carry on with the job." He slid the decoder across the desk, closer to me, and I picked it up and tucked it away. I was shocked he would just give me the decoder for the will like that. Didn't it basically act like a key to all the information on the operation? I think he could tell I was surprised because he explained himself.

"Your parents were my father's closest friends. I spent a lot of time with them growing up and they are some of the most loyal and trustworthy people I know. I'm choosing to trust you with this because I trust them."

I nodded, my heart full of emotion. It sounded like he knew my parents better than I did. "Also, between you and me, both Harrison and Huxley are stupid. I only have them here to do the dirty work, like the kids. They wouldn't be able to carry this operation on if something happened to me." I nodded again, starting to understand where he was coming from.

"If something happens to me, go to your parents and get them to help you," he said, looking me directly in the eye.

"I will," I responded. "Thank you for trusting me with this." I got up to leave.

The next morning, we left for the first city and the start of our journey.

30

Meg

From the security recordings, I was able to figure out that the white convertible had gotten to the parking lot at 8:17 that morning. There was a male driver who never got out of the car, so I wasn't able to get a good look at his face. I assumed he was either Cain or someone who worked for him. After the car parked, three kids got out. One of them was Lizzie and one was Noah. They had different hair colors (probably wigs) and they had some extra birthmarks and things like that, but I was sure it was them. I wasn't sure who the third kid was.

Originally when I had heard there were three kids that came into the prison, I assumed the third one was one of Cain's men, but based on how Lizzie and Noah were acting around her, it made me think she was more of their friend than their enemy. I ran a facial recognition scan on her with my laptop and the results showed that her name was Nolly Prescot. I had heard that name before. With a start, I remembered that Nolly was Lizzie's best friend. Lizzie would talk about her all the time.

Was Nolly kidnapped too and it just hadn't been reported? Or had she gone along willingly? I decided to do a background check on her and her family. The results were shocking. According to the database, Nolly's parents, James and Lyn Prescot, had been suspected of being smugglers who had worked with Cain's father. They had just never been caught. No one had been able to find a solid connection between them and Cain father or any evidence that was strong enough to put them behind bars. They had done a good job of covering their tracks, so the authorities were forced to let them go.

But now Nolly was working with Cain? There was no way that was a coincidence. She was probably helping him, but it hadn't looked like Lizzie and Noah knew that. They were treating her like their friend. She had to be going behind their backs and working for Cain. That was horrible. What kind of friend does that?

Turing my attention back to the video, I looked for anything else that could give me a lead as to their location or their future plans. Thankfully, I was able to see the license plate number on the car. That was huge. I ran it through the database, and it said that the car belonged to a woman named Sally Lue. I knew that was a pretty stupid name, so I figured that it was most likely made up. The car was registered to an address though, 103 Briar-Bush Drive. I looked up the property and saw that it was an empty patch of land. In Wyoming. Definitely not helpful.

I decided to use a different approach and use traffic cameras to follow the car. I followed it and saw that it had gone to a secluded area downtown. The driver got out and made a phone call. Unfortunately, he was facing towards the ground the whole time, so I still couldn't get a good look at his face.

Eventually, he got back into the car, and they drove to a decrepit looking building. I had a hard time figuring out what it was until I spotted a sign that said MARCUS LAW FIRM. Looks like that was going to be my next stop.

I drove over to the law office and got out of my car, hoping to find more answers. The building was really sketchy. It had bars over the windows and the paint on the outside was peeling. I walked up to the door and went inside, feeling very unwelcome. I wasn't sure the best way to go about this. Whoever Bill and Cain's lawyer was, I was sure they weren't exactly a law-abiding citizen. They probably were very unlikely to give me the answers I needed, and I was sure that showing them my badge wouldn't help. All I really needed to know was what Cain's man had gone there for, and I thought I knew what it was. He had learned someone had died then when to a law firm. I was pretty sure he wanted to look at Bill Smith's will. I decided to just ask the secretary and see what happened.

I walked up to her desk, and she said, "How may I help you today?"

"Hi," I replied trying to be friendly. "Has anyone been in here today asking to see Bill Smith's will?" I figured I might as well just go for it.

"Maybe," she replied, sounding skeptical. "Why do you need to know?"

"Oh, I was just wondering," I said, trying to sound innocent. The secretary was definitely not buying it.

"May I see the will," I asked.

"No," she said bluntly. "The will is only able to be viewed by beneficiaries right now." That gave me an idea. Nolly's parents had worked will Bill, so maybe they were listed as beneficiaries. It was a long shot, but I tried anyways.

"I think I am a beneficiary," I said. "My name is Lyn Prescot."

"Lyn Prescot?" she asked, still sounding suspicious. "Let

me go ask the lawyers." She walked out from behind the desk and went down a hallway. I stood there waiting, trying to stand still. So far, my plan was working. I had to play it cool though because of she got any more suspicious, I could kiss seeing that will goodbye.

A few minutes later, she came back. "Well, Mrs. Prescot, you are one of the beneficiaries," she said, sounding mildly surprised. "You can make your way back there to the office at the end of the hall." I breathed a sigh of relief as I turned to go down the hallway. I walked to the end and knocked on a brown wooden door.

"Come in," said a rough voice. I opened the door and stepped into a shabby office. The desk in the center was old and chipped and all three chairs in the room were falling apart. Behind the desk sitting in one of the chairs was an equally shabby looking man. He was wearing a suit that was clearly very old, and he had a shaggy look about him. He had dark eyes and a scar that ran down his face.

"Hello, Mrs. Prescot," he said.

"Hello, Sir," I replied trying not to show how much his appearance unnerved me.

"The will is on the table, take as long as you need," he said, then walked out of the room. Anxious to get out of there, I snapped a picture of each page of the will, then left the office, went back down the hall, through the lobby, and back into my car.

Now that I had the pictures of the will, I really wasn't sure what to do with them. I read through the will, but nothing seemed out of the ordinary. I was sure if Cain needed it, it had to be important. I decided to hold off on the will for now and go back to following the white convertible though traffic light camera footage.

I followed the car as far as the cameras covered. I tracked it out to the Interstate. I was really hoping that their hide-out or wherever they were wasn't too far away because I was about to go pay a visit to all the properties off the Interstate. Thankfully, this area was mostly empty country, but there were still enough properties around to make me look like an idiot driving around checking them all.

Already dreading what felt like a wild goose chase, I left the law office parking lot and drove until I got to the point where the cameras stopped. I started looking for properties and the first one I saw was a small white house. I pulled into the driveway and knocked on the door.

An old woman with gray hair and a kind smile opened it. "Hello, Ma'am," I said. "I'm looking for a group of missing teenagers. Have you seen or heard anything?"

"Missing teenagers?" she asked, worriedly. "No, I haven't heard anything." Then, she turned around, went to her living room and crouched down on her knees in front of her couch. Confused, I slowly followed her in through the open front door.

"Um, Ma'am?" I asked. I could hear her mumbling, but I couldn't make out the words.

Then she said, "Amen," and got up.

Realizing, she was so disturbed by the news of missing teenagers she had decided to pray. I said, "Thank you," then, "Would you mind if I looked around a little bit?" She shook her head no, and I searched the house.

I found absolutely nothing. Not that I was expecting to. When I turned to thank her for her time, she grabbed my hand and said in a soft voice, "Please find them."

Her sincerity and care for others brought tears to my eyes.

"I'll do my absolute best," I whispered. She nodded and I left. Her concern for them made me realize even more how important it was that I succeeded in finding them.

The next few properties weren't as eventful. One was a completely abandoned barn. I met a few other people whose houses I searched to find nothing. Many of the properties off the highway were down long gravel driveways, so anytime I saw some kind of road or path leading away from the highway, I took it. Sometimes, it would dead end in the forest, but even then, I would get out and look around.

I had been searching for at least six hours and it was almost midnight by the time I found a small building that seemed to be falling apart. I had taken a small path off the highway that I had almost missed. The path had hit a dead end in the forest, but I got out and looked around anyway shining my flashlight through the trees. I was about to give up and get back in my car, when I saw a flash of white, which turned out to be a building. I walked up to it, but it looked deserted. Except for the small white car in the driveway. A white car that had the same license plate as the car I had been following all day!

Growing excited, I walked around the perimeter of the property, checking for any signs of people or signs of a trap before I went inside. Thankfully, I saw no one. Then, I jumped the fence surrounding the area and went inside the large concrete building. It was just an empty space.

Getting discouraged, I decided to look around anyway. I went to the back corner and started walking back and forth, sweeping my flashlight across the room as I did so. The light from my flashlight glinted off something metal on the floor which caught my attention. I went to get a closer look and realized it was a hinge to a trap door! I pulled it open and went down the ladder.

At the bottom there was a common area with two hallways branching off. I looked around the common area and still saw no one. It was really strange. Either no one was there at the moment, or they had moved on already. Still, I had to make sure. I searched the place.

I found a room that looked like an office and finally found Cain's fingerprints. This was it! The place I had been searching for without a doubt. I knew there had to be more leads here. I found a room that had to be a cell. It had four pairs of handcuffs, but it looked like only three were used. I found the fingerprints of Nolly, Noah, and Lizzie, exactly what I was looking for. And then I noticed blood. Blood surrounded by Noah's fingerprints.

I had to sit down. My friend's blood was being shed, and it was my job to stop it. That thought terrified me. I hadn't known Lizzie that well, but she had gone to my school and Noah was the closest thing I ever had to a boyfriend and the way he looked at me in the hallway on my last day of normalcy was warm and caring. I desperately hoped he was alright. I could feel myself spiraling even as I was trying to hold myself together. "But, wait," I thought. His blood was saying something! It looked like he had written something in his blood. Three letters, clear as day. NYC. A perfect clue! Guess I was headed to New York City.

31

Lizzie

pparently, we were headed to the Big Apple, but, I mean, who knew if we really were? I had no reason to trust anything Cain said. I just couldn't believe he was getting away with this! I also couldn't believe no one had found us yet. It felt like we had been missing for weeks, even though it had really only been a few days. I was usually the type of person who looked on the bright side, but I was starting to worry that we might not be found. I didn't want to know what would happen to us when we got to the end of this whole thing. What would Cain do with us when he decided he didn't need us anymore? It was a scary thought.

I was so sick of being worried and scared and being forced to help someone break the law. This whole being kidnapped thing was no fun at all. I knew Noah felt the same way that I did. I could see the constant frustration on his face, and I could tell that he was determined to find a way out of here. He was optimistic that someone was going to follow our trail and find us, and he was determined to do anything he could to help them.

Before we left the hideout, Cain and his kidnapper friends had come into the cell to untie us. Noah had mouthed off to them, saying they were never going to get away with what they were doing and that what they were doing was evil and terrible and all sorts of things. I don't know if he needed to let off some steam or if it was part of some plan of his, but either way, he made Cain mad enough that Cain came over to him and dragged his nails down Noah's arm that had been cut earlier. It looked really painful, and it started bleeding, but Noah didn't even cry out; he just glared at Cain.

Cain then left the room and let his kidnapper buddies finish untying us. They untied Noah and Nolly first, then moved on to me. Once Noah was untied and the kidnappers' backs were turned, I saw him start messing with his blood and smearing it on the floor. When I realized he was writing "NYC." I understood his plan. It was so genius to leave behind clues. Then, I got really nervous that the kidnappers would see it before we left. Thankfully, as soon as I was untied, they escorted us out of the room and into a car.

I was glad Noah and I were on the same page about escaping, but I wasn't sure about Nolly. Every time I tried to talk to her, she would give short responses or ignore me all together. I wasn't sure if she was just in shock because of the whole situation or what, but something was off about her.

"Only about an hour left now," Noah whispered to me, pulling me from my thoughts. "I heard Huxley tell Cain."

"Thanks," I whispered in response, thankful the ride was coming to an end. We had been driving for hours and my body was all stiff. I looked out the windows at the trees we were passing as they slowly began to turn into buildings that got taller and taller. It looked like we were headed to New York City after all.

We drove across a bridge and saw the city in all its glory. New York was beautiful. Some of the buildings were so tall you could barely see their tops. As we drove through the city, I just became more and more amazed. The store fronts were beautifully decorated and there were so many people walking around. There were displays talking about the city's history and street vendors selling everything from hot dogs to handmade scarves. We drove past a beautiful ice-skating rink with a huge golden statue in the front of it. Next to the statue, there was a huge Christmas tree.

"Why is there a Christmas tree?" I blurted out.

Noah was kind enough to reply. "Christmas is only a little over a month away," he said. That surprised me. I had lost all concept of time since being kidnapped. I couldn't believe Christmas was so soon. What if we didn't make it home before then?

I looked out the window again and tried to focus on the people ice-skating. There was an elderly couple skating past, holding hands. There was a mom and dad trying to teach a little kid to skate. There were people taking a family photo in front of the statue. A tear rolled down my face. Seeing all the people on the ice-skating rink having fun with their loved ones made me remember how much I missed my own family. We kept driving past the ice-skating rink, and I wiped my eyes. I was not going to sit here and cry. I was going to get home.

We kept driving through the bustling city of lights and into a small, rundown neighborhood. All of the houses seemed to be in some sort of disrepair with cracked windows, missing bricks, caved-in sections of roof, or broken front doors. We pulled up and stopped in front of a brown house with a front porch that had a sagging awning, like it was going to cave in at any point.

"Kids? Get out and go into the house," Cain instructed, getting straight to the point and handing Nolly the keys. "Go inside, and in the dining room under the rug there is a sliding panel. Open it and then get the book that's inside and bring it to me. Do not open it. If you are not back within six minutes, there will be consequences. Go."

We scrambled out of the car and up to the front door of the house. Nolly turned the key, and we hurried inside. The inside was worse than the outside. The house looked like it used to be really nice, but it had been neglected for too long. A chandelier had fallen from the ceiling, the paint on the walls was peeling, and all the furniture had holes in it. This wasn't really what I had pictured an evil lair to look like, but, oh well.

Not wanting to experience the "consequences" Cain was talking about, we hurried to a room with a once fancy light fixture and a big table, what would have been a nice dining room back in the day. Noah pushed the table over, and I rolled back the rug. Then, we both got down on our hands and knees and felt around for the panel. There were no windows, making the room nearly pitch black, and we had no flashlight, so we were having a hard time finding the panel.

"Nolly! Help us find it!" I yelled, worried we were running out of time. Nolly was just standing in the doorway looking at something in the hallway.

"I don't want to get dirty," she complained. "These jeans were expensive and . . ."

Really?? I thought. Why in the world was she worrying about her fancy-schmancy clothes when so much else was happening right now? I would have yelled at her except Noah started talking.

"Never mind, I found it," he said, also sounding annoyed. What was going on with that girl? Noah opened the panel, grabbed the book, and we all ran back outside. As we hopped back in the car, Cain said, "Just in time."

"Here you go!" said Nolly, snatching the book from Noah. I looked at Nolly questioningly, wondering why she took the book, but she wasn't looking at me.

"We are staying here for the night," Cain said, taking the book and starting to flip through it.

If we were staying there for the night, why on earth had he just made us freak out about getting the book to him? What kind of person threatens people and makes them worry for no reason? I guess the same kind of people that kidnap innocent kids. Cain pulled the car behind the house, and we all got out. We followed the kidnappers into the house and into another small, windowless room with a dead bolt on the door.

"You'll sleep here," the kidnapper said then left, turning the deadbolt behind him.

32

Noah

I was too restless to sleep. All I had done was ride in the car all day, so I wasn't very tired. And I was trying to sleep on the rock-hard floor with no blankets or pillows. But I felt like something good had come of this day. I had been able to leave that clue behind this morning. I knew that it was a long shot but relying on those long shots was all I really had. I just knew someone had to be looking for us. They just had to have someone on our case somewhere.

Deep down, I hoped it was Meg, even though that didn't really make sense, but I was positive it was her I saw in that parking lot at the prison. And if I recognized her with different hair, maybe she recognized me in disguise too. Even if she wasn't a secret agent or anything, maybe she heard that we were missing and reported that she saw us. My theory had a lot of maybes and far-fetched explanations, but I just had to believe someone was out there looking for us, getting closer and closer to finding us. And it was my job to do whatever I could to help that person get us out of here.

I was even more restless now. I glanced around the room to

see if anyone else was still awake. Lizzie was out, but Nolly just sat and stared at the wall. She wasn't even trying to sleep. She had been acting really weird. Like today when she took the book out of my hand to give to Cain. It was like she was trying to impress him. Was she hoping she could butter him up enough that he would let her go?

I didn't know and trying to figure her out was just frustrating me, so I rolled over and tried to fall asleep. An hour or so later, I was still awake when I heard the sounds outside the door. I rolled to face it, but kept my eyes mostly closed so it would look like I was asleep.

Harrison opened the door and came inside. After looking at Lizzie and me for a minute (checking to make sure we were asleep, I think), Nolly stood up and left with him. *What?* She had kind-of acted like she knew he was coming for her, sitting up and not trying to sleep. I was pretty sure by that point that she was a traitor. Why else would she leave with Harrison? And her being a traitor would explain why she felt like she didn't have to look for the book with us and why she wanted to impress Cain. I didn't want to jump to conclusions like that and think the worst about her, but it made sense.

Then I realized she had left her jacket in the room. I decided to search it. It was a risky move, but maybe there was something in there that would prove she was a traitor. Or maybe there was something that would help Lizzie and me escape. Since I was also relying on the theory that some government agent was out looking for us, I had to check the jacket and see if I could find another clue to leave behind and continue the trail. This could be my only chance.

I slowly snuck over to her side of the room and lifted the corner of her jacket. I looked through the front pockets and found nothing but a gum wrapper. Then I checked the inside pockets. Bingo! There was a disk that had letters and words on it. It looked like something you would see in a spy movie that would help the spies communicate without other people knowing what they were saying. A decoder!

Then, I heard footsteps. I dropped the decoder hurried back over to my spot and lay down, again pretending to be asleep. Huxley came in and picked up Nolly's jacket. He glanced around the room then left. I waited for a few minutes to be sure no one else was coming then I looked at the decoder again. At least, I was pretty sure that's what it was.

I didn't know whether to be thrilled or upset. On one hand, I was excited to have information that could be helpful and have a way to leave a trail. On the other, I couldn't believe Nolly was a traitor. Before all this, I hadn't really known her or Lizzie that well, but I had thought they were best friends. And to think I used to *like* Nolly! I was disgusted.

Realizing I was now way too wired to try to sleep, I decided to try and find a way to leave the decoder behind. I lay there, trying to come up with a way to leave it without anyone noticing, when the doorknob turned again. Nolly came in, then the door closed and locked behind her. She had a little smile on her face, then she lay down and turned over.

This was infuriating. I was so mad that she was going behind our backs and helping Cain, I almost confronted her about it right then and there, but thankfully I was able to calm down. I knew that it was to our advantage if Lizzie and I knew that she was a traitor, but she didn't know we knew.

Realizing it was late and finally getting tired because of this emotional roller coaster, I rolled over and eventually fell into a fitful sleep. The next morning, I left my jacket in the room on purpose and made it all the way outside before "remembering" and going back inside to get it. I grabbed my jacket and left the decoder on the floor, hoping someone would find it.

33

Nolly

In the car the next day on the way to the next stop, I couldn't stop thinking about the previous night. I had stayed awake, hoping to be able to talk to Cain when Harrison finally came to get me. I followed him into a parlor, or what used to be a parlor, and sat down on a couch across from Cain who was sitting in an armchair that was slightly falling apart.

The room had peeling wallpaper, a chandelier with all the bulbs blown out, and a bookshelf filled with moldy books. Clearly, this had been a nice place once, but now it was just revolting. I saw a dead rat on my way to the parlor and I literally gagged. I couldn't wait to move on from here.

"You called?" I said jokingly.

"Any updates?" he asked, not glancing up from the laptop he was working on.

"No, nothing at all," I said, slightly annoyed. "Do you have any updates for me? I'm not just your little minion. I want the details." If he thought he was just going to be able to order me around, he was very wrong. He studied me for a moment with that same expression of deciding whether or not to trust me. I don't know why he still had second thoughts about me. Hadn't I proved myself?

"Sure, I'll tell you what's in the book," he finally said nonchalantly. "But let's go outside so we have a bit more privacy."

"I'll need my jacket," I replied, getting up to go get it.

"Huxley, go get her jacket," Cain said to one of his cronies. Huxley left the room to go get my jacket and Cain went back to working on his laptop. Well, this was boring.

"Whatcha working on?" I asked Cain, curious about what he was doing but more so about how much he trusted me.

"Nothing," Cain replied, closing his laptop. Apparently, I didn't have all his trust yet. I would just have to work harder. I'm not sure why gaining his trust was so important to me. Maybe it's because if I impressed him and got him to really trust me as a partner, it would impress my parents. Maybe they would finally see me and appreciate me.

Cain checked his watch then said, "It's getting late. Let's go head outside. Huxley can bring you your jacket out there."

"Fine by me," I said, getting off the moldy couch. Cain and I left the parlor and walked outside into the cold and windy night.

"So why exactly does this give us more privacy," I asked, shivering.

"It can be very easy to pretend to be asleep and then try to eavesdrop on conversations. And I don't really like calling you out in the middle of the night anyways because I'm afraid it may raise suspicions, but it's really my only option. My plan is to talk to the others in the middle of the night too just to make sure they aren't onto us." That was actually a really good plan, but I wasn't about to tell him that. My goal was to impress him, not flatter him. He didn't need any ego boosters. Just then, Huckleberry, or whatever his crony's name was, came out with my jacket.

"Here you go," he said gruffly. As he was handing me the jacket, the wind caught it, and it blew out into the middle of the road.

"Huxley, you stupid, go get that jacket!" Cain said angrily. Huxley ran out to the road, picked up my jacket, and brought it to me.

"Sorry, Miss," he said, then scurried inside, probably to escape anymore of Cain's wrath.

Putting my jacket on, I realized my pocket was empty. "Cain, the decoder! It isn't here!" I exclaimed. "I've been keeping it in my pocket, but I think it blew away!"

"Ugh, stupid Huxley!" Cain responded, obviously fed up. "I cannot find good help. The only reason I have these two around is because their parents worked for my dad. I'm so close to just getting rid of them both."

"Do we need to go try to find it?" I asked.

He thought about it for a minute. "No, it's fine," he said. "It's so windy it's probably already gone. Plus, anyone around here who finds it won't know what to do with it and will most likely throw it away. And even if they do realize what it is, they'll have no clue what it decodes."

I breathed a sigh of relief. I knew it was the stupid crony's fault, but I was still worried that if Cain was mad, some of the blame might fall on me. Trying to impress Cain was really starting to wear on me.

"So, tell me about this book then," I said, ready to move on to a different topic and get out of the cold weather.

"It has all of the instructions for how to run the printing

press," Cain explained. "It's basically a step-by-step manual for how to print the counterfeit money."

Interested, I asked, "Can I see it?"

"No."

Did he just tell me, No? After everything I was trying to do to impress him, did he really just tell me, No? I was fed up. Deciding that he needed a piece of my mind, I said, "Look, Cain. I am not here to work for you. I want to be your equal in this whole scheme. I am risking just as much as you, maybe even more because I am a double-agent, and I want to be treated as such. You better start telling me things and I better stop having to ask for information. If you can't do that, I can very well leave."

He stared at me for a second, then he smiled. "You sure have spunk," he said, "just like your mom." My mom? I was like my mom? "When her and your dad would come visit, she would always tell these crazy stories about their schemes, and she was always the hero. She stood up for herself and demanded what she wanted. She was quite a force to be reckoned with. I can see you get that from her . . . and I will start including you as much as I can . . . partner."

That was quite possibly the nicest thing anyone had ever said to me. I was like my mother. There was no one else that I looked up to more and to be told that I had some of her qualities was just . . . perfect. It made me think that this whole scheme was worth it. Hearing that story though also made me sad. It reminded me of how little I really knew my parents. I didn't know my mother was like that and I had never heard one of her stories like Cain had.

Cain then handed me the book, bringing me out of my thoughts. I glanced through it seeing instructions and diagrams and a bunch of mechanical and scientific mumbo-jumbo I didn't really understand. I thought about trying to ask Cain to explain it, but then the cold weather and late hour got to me, so I decided it was probably time to head in. I handed Cain back the book and we turned to go inside.

On our way in, I turned to look at Cain. "Thanks," I said.

"Anytime, Partner," he replied.

While we were on the road the next day, this scene was replaying in my head, and I was thinking about my parents, my new partnership with Cain, and of course, how much money we would eventually make. At one point in the ride, Lizzie asked me how I was doing. After a little bit of fabulous acting, I got her off my case. I knew that we used to be best friends, but I was moving onto better things with Cain now. Glancing between the two, I knew I had made the right choice in following Cain.

34

Meg

As I was getting closer to my destination, I retraced my steps. Earlier that morning, it had looked like I had just missed them leaving for New York. The tire tracks in the mud were still fresh and Noah's blood wasn't completely dry.

I headed (speeding slightly) in the direction of the Big Apple, trying to make up for the extra 30 minutes I estimated I was behind them. On my way there, I sent Kat an update, including pictures of the will and the "note," I guess you could call it, that Noah had left for me.

When I got to New York, I headed over to the less developed and more criminal area of the city. I was going to check out a small neighborhood that Cain's father had been spotted in multiple times, according to my case file. It was suspected that Cain's dad had a house in the neighborhood, but no one was sure which house it was. I figured if Cain was anywhere in NYC that was where he'd be.

It was nearly 11 o'clock, so everyone was probably getting ready for bed or already asleep, which would not help me to see if the houses were occupied or not. I drove down the street in the neighborhood where Cain's father had been spotted all those years ago but didn't see anything out of the ordinary. However, if Cain was in New York, he was almost certainly in this neighborhood. I would have to wait till morning to see if I could find him.

Deciding it was best to settle in for the night, I drove my car to the end of the road and turned it off. I would be sleeping in the car tonight. I was laying down trying to fall asleep when the tears came.

All the stress of the past couple of days was catching up to me as I had known it would. I knew I wasn't made for this job; it wasn't me. At the beginning of this case, I had tried to convince myself that I could do this, but all the stress and playing tough guy? I hated it. And the more blood I saw and the more danger I thought Lizzie and Noah were in, the worse everything got. If something happened and I failed, I don't know if I'd be able to live with myself. If I didn't know the people who were in this case, I would be tempted to quit. But, because the kids in danger were people I knew, I had to keep going. I was just so unbearably worried about them.

Especially Noah. I couldn't explain it, my feelings for him. In a way he had been with me my whole journey. From being the last person I saw at school to now giving me clues to help me solve this case. Interacting with him again made me remember everything I liked about him freshman year. His smile, his strength, his determination . . . My last thoughts were of Noah as I drifted off to sleep.

* * *

The next morning, I woke up at 5 AM, hoping to see Cain. I was almost positive he would show up and visit his dad's old house, but if he didn't I wasn't sure what I was going to do. I hoped that I would be able to catch the license plate number of the car he was in, so I could find them later. Then, I wanted to search whatever house he went in. I wasn't just going to follow him because I didn't want him to get suspicious. Plus, I had orders not to take him in until he led me to the location of his father's bunker. That way, we could shut it down once and for all.

At 7 AM a black SUV pulled away from one of the houses. The driver was male and looked similar to the person that had driven the white convertible to the jail and law office. The person in the passenger seat was definitely Cain. There were also what looked like 2 girls and a boy in the backseat. I knew that had to be them. I snapped a picture of the license plate, then waited for them to drive away.

I went over to the house that the car came from and found the back door unlocked. Strange. I walked inside and started to look around. The house was falling apart, so I was trying to be careful. I came to an empty room with a deadbolt lock on the door and nothing at all inside. I was about to turn around when I noticed something on the ground. I bent down and picked it up. Thanks to my training, I recognized what it was immediately: A decoder! For what though? And how did it get here?

My first thought was Noah. Maybe he left it for me to find. I took a picture of it and sent it to Kat. Kat would know how to read it and what it meant. Or she would be able to find people that did.

I decided to finish searching the rest of the house, hoping to find another clue. I found Cain, Nolly, Lizzie, and Noah's fingerprints, but really nothing else interesting.

Right when I finished searching the house, I got a call from Kat. "Hey, Kat!" I said, picking up the phone. "You got anything for me?"

"Meg, you wouldn't believe it! I was going through the will you sent me, and I realized it wasn't written like a traditional will would be written. There was just something off. Then, I got the picture of the decoder. I thought maybe the two went together, so I sent the pictures of the will and decoder over to one of my friends who specializes in codes to see if they could see anything else written in the will!"

"And?" I asked, getting excited.

"And they did! They said the will has the instructions on how to get the key to the bunker and the bunker itself!"

"Oh, my goodness!" I exclaimed, flooded with relief. "That's exactly what I needed to hear!"

"I'll text you the decoded version of the will as soon as I can. Just keep following the plan. You got this, Meg. I believe in you." Kat was just the best.

"Thank you, Kat," I replied, "for the help and the vote of confidence." This was it. I knew where I needed to go and what I needed to do. I was going to be able to do this after all.

35

Lizzie

We were headed to Washington, D.C., and despite the fact that I was being taken there against my will, I was excited. I had always wanted to see The Capitol, the historic buildings, the beautiful landmarks, and the place where all the important decisions for our country are made. It was also the place where some of the most amazing debates had taken place. I had always wanted to come watch while the Senate or the House of Representatives was in session. Not that I would get to do that this time around, but maybe I would get to see the outside of The Congress Building.

Cain had said that the ride would take about four hours, but I couldn't sleep, so I just stared out the window, watching the world go by. At one point in the ride, when Nolly was sleeping, Noah whispered to me, "Hey, I need to tell you something."

"What?" I whispered back. Cain was in the front, listening to my kidnapper and the other guy talk. They were in the middle row with Nolly. Noah and I were all the way in the back. I was pretty sure we'd be good to talk, as long as we whispered.

"It's about Nolly," Noah started. "I think she's working with them," he said.

"What??" I whisper-yelled, shocked.

"Shhh," Noah said, looking towards the front of the SUV to make sure we weren't heard. "Remember how Cain gave her the key when we went into the house? And how she didn't help us look for the book yesterday? And last night, I couldn't fall asleep, and I saw her leave the room with one of the guys. Then, when she came back, she was smiling. I know y'all were friends, so you know her better, but that's what I saw."

I let that sink in. Nolly? A traitor? There was no way! We were friends! She would never betray me like that . . . Or would she? I mean, I knew our relationship had been rocky over the past couple of months, but was it rocky enough for her to betray me like this? I couldn't exactly argue with what Noah had seen, but, for me at least, it wasn't enough to be sure she was a traitor. What he saw was very suspicious, but also very circumstantial.

"Wow," was all I ended up saying in reply. I wasn't really sure what to think, let alone say.

"Do you believe me?" asked Noah. I looked across the car at Nolly, then back at Noah. Over the past couple of days, I had grown to trust Noah, maybe more than I did Nolly. Something about being in a life-or-death situation, I guess. But that still couldn't undo a friendship dating back to elementary school.

"Honestly, Noah," I said. "I know that all of that looks bad, but it doesn't necessarily mean she's with them. Just because Cain handed her the key doesn't mean she's a traitor; she might've just been the one nearest to him at the time. And she is really picky about her clothes, which I know doesn't make any sense, but that's just how she is. It made me mad, too, that she didn't look for the book, but I don't think she would betray me like that."

Noah sighed. I could tell I didn't convince him. "Well, what about her leaving in the middle of the night last night?" he whispered.

"Maybe Cain is going to talk to each of us at night and Nolly was just the first one," I suggested. That thought scared me. Having a one-on-one with Cain in the middle of the night? Please, no. But it was a better alternative to my best friend betraying me. "She's my best friend, Noah, I need more proof than that," I said.

Noah sighed again. "Look, Lizzie," he said. "I know this is hard for you, but I really think Nolly is working with them. Last night, while she was gone, I searched her jacket. I found a little disk with words and letters on it, like the kind they have in spy movies that solve codes. I don't know where else she would have gotten it unless Cain gave it to her."

What? I was really trying to give my best friend the benefit of the doubt here, but it was getting harder and harder. Why would she have something like that? "Maybe she stole it?" I suggested.

"Then why wouldn't she tell us?" Noah asked patiently. "And when would she have done it? We were together all the time. The only time she could have gotten it was at night when we are sleeping. And she wouldn't be able to steal it at night because we are always locked up."

Noah was right. The only way for Nolly to have the decoder was for Cain to give it to her. I just didn't want to believe it. How could my best friend be helping the man that kidnapped me?

"Do you believe me now?" Noah asked gently. I looked over at Nolly and back at Noah again. During this whole mess, Nolly had been nothing but distant while Noah had been helpful, caring, and working to get us out of here.

"Yeah, I do," I said with a sigh. "I guess Nolly really is working with them. "What should we do?"

"I don't know," he replied. "Maybe we should just not talk about important things in front of her. I feel like it may be dangerous if they know we know that she's a traitor." I understood what Noah was saying, but part of me wanted to confront Nolly and ask her why she did it. Why would she do this to me? Our friendship had been struggling, but didn't all the time we spent together since that day in fourth grade mean anything to her? But, in the end, I agreed with Noah. We needed to stay quiet and patient and do anything we could to gain an upper hand.

I spent the rest of the car ride continuing to stare out the window, looking at nothing. We drove through the capital, but I was too distracted by thoughts of Nolly to really pay attention to any of the sights we were driving past. I just couldn't believe it.

Eventually, Cain barked out, "Everyone awake? We're almost there." We drove into a neighborhood that resembled the one we had been in earlier that day: run-down, dingy, and pretty darn sketchy.

We turned a corner and passed a car that was stopped at a stop sign. The car caught my attention because it looked pretty new and nice and not at all like it belonged in the neighborhood. I looked at the driver, and she looked awfully familiar. I nudged Noah and motioned for him to look out the window. He did, and his face lit up. He must have thought the driver was who I thought she was. *Meg?* I mouthed to him. He nodded, trying to suppress a smile. That crazy theory we had turned out to be true. What other explanation would make sense? How did she get here? I had no idea. But the fact that she was here was all that mattered. Seeing her brought me so much hope. For the first time since this whole disaster started, I thought that a happy ending was possible.

36

Nolly

As we drove along the coast on our way to DC, I pretended to be asleep. My main job on this mission was to spy on Lizzie and Noah after all, and, like Cain had mentioned the night before, it was very easy to eavesdrop by pretending to be asleep. Plus, now that Cain and I were partners, I had to be sure I was pulling my own weight. I had to keep impressing him.

It was quiet for most of the drive, but then, Noah started to talk to Lizzie. It was kind-of difficult to hear, but I could make out enough to realize they were talking about me. It seemed like Noah was saying something bad about me, but Lizzie was defending me. That really was sweet of her, but seriously? Was she still holding on to that "best friends forever" thing? She needed to grow up. I certainly had.

I kept trying to listen to their conversation, but I was only getting little snippets of it. I shifted the position I was fake-sleeping in and suddenly I could hear Lizzie loud and clear. "I guess Nolly really is working with them."

What?? Noah had told her I was a traitor? They were on to

me! How did they know? This was bad. I needed to tell Cain. All of these thoughts started to swirl through my head at once, sending me into a full-blown panic. I had failed. My one job was to spy on them, and my cover had just been blown. I was a failure. No one would be proud of me now. Cain and I wouldn't be partners and my parents would just be disappointed when they heard about all that had happened.

How was I going to tell Cain? I was just going to have to rip it off like a band-aid. He had to have known I wouldn't be able to stay undercover forever. And he had played a part in blowing my cover, what with pulling me out in the middle of the night. It wasn't my fault. I would just let him know that. It would all be fine. He wouldn't be mad, and we could still be partners. I would still make my parents proud. Or at least that's what I told myself as we drove through the streets of Washington, D.C.

Finally, we drove away from The Capital and into a small dingy neighborhood like the last one. The disgustingness of the area was so bad it distracted me from my thoughts of telling Cain what just happened. Boy, Cain's dad really had no style. With his whole fake money scheme, I would have thought he could have afforded to live somewhere a bit classier. We pulled up to another dumpy house with broken windows, graffitied walls, and a dead tree in the front yard.

"Everyone out," Cain barked from the front seat. We all filed out of the car and walked into the house into what looked like a living room. A living room with moldy carpet, no furniture, and a burnt-out light fixture. Again, Cain's dad really knew how to decorate a house.

Noah and Lizzie went in first and I followed, first whispering to Cain, "They are onto me." Hopefully, that would get the message across, and at least now, in front of everyone, he probably wouldn't yell at me.

Once in the room, Cain looked around then said, "Sit," and left, probably looking for the key that was supposedly hidden here. We all sat down on the threadbare carpet waiting in silence for a couple of minutes before hearing a roar of outrage. Cain ran back into the room clearly trying to compose himself. His usually calm face was flushed and blotchy. His hair was all messed up and he was breathing heavily.

"Nolly, come here," he said. I got up and walked over to him, worried. This was it. He was going to yell at me. I was going to be completely humiliated, then tossed into the streets. I was never going to make anyone proud or get to be anyone's partner in anything. I turned to look at him, the fear in my eyes definitely showing.

But then, instead of totally chewing me out, he turned to address Noah and Lizzie. "So, you've figured it out. Your friend's a traitor. I'm going to talk to her for a second and you two Will. Not. Move."

Cain grabbed my hand and took me to another room. My temporary relief instantly vanished. Apparently, he just wanted to yell at me in private. I winced waiting for him to start going at it when he said, "The decoder."

"Wait, what?" I said, confused. "What's going on? Are you mad at me?" I asked, spitting the questions out.

"The decoder," Cain repeated. "I don't think it blew away in the wind. One of them stole it from your pocket and passed it on to someone who I'm assuming is following us. Since you had the decoder, that's probably how they figured out you are helping me. They must have put two and two together and figured it out. Also, whoever they gave the decoder to got a copy of the will somehow and got here before us. They took the key to the bunker."

"Oh, my gosh," I gasped. I stared at him in shock. I had thought we were doing so well. The idea of having to face actual punishment and the fact that we were actually committing a crime had never really seemed real until now.

"People are following us?" I asked.

"Yes, most likely government agents trying to catch me. Your friends did a good job of tipping them off. They probably did everything while you were sleeping."

I couldn't believe it. "I'm so sorry," I whispered, trying not to cry.

Cain studied me for a moment, then said. "It's fine. It's partly my fault because I gave you the decoder. I'm not mad at you. Who I am mad at, however, are your little friends."

I was relieved. I could still do this, could still make my family proud. I looked up at Cain. "What do we do now?" I asked.

"Well," he started. "The good news is that I have a backup key to the bunker. I found it in a secret compartment in my father's desk. I wanted to come here to make sure he didn't leave anything other than the key and to get this key to prevent anyone else from having access to the bunker. Obviously, the second part failed, so the next step is to get to the bunker before whoever got the other key does. But first, I'm still angry. Your little friends are in trouble. And they now have to face the consequences."

37

Noah

As soon as Nolly left the room, Lizzie asked me, "Noah? Do you know what's going on?"

I replied softly, trying to prepare her for what I knew was coming. Or at least what I thought. All I had was a theory and it was a theory that leaned more on hope than facts, but I was still pretty sure it was correct.

"You know how at the beginning of all this we were wondering if maybe Meg or someone else was trying to save us?" I started.

Lizzie nodded, eyes wide. "Yeah, because we didn't really think she was looking for us at the beginning, but we just saw her, so . . ."

"Right. I thought she, or someone else had been trying to help us, and seeing her just now proved that." I hadn't even started to process what seeing Meg meant. I knew it meant that she really had been following us and that seeing her at the prison wasn't just a coincidence. I was trying to convince myself that the reason I was so excited that I had seen her was because it meant that there was definitely someone out there trying to save us. But there was something else under that excitement, something that suggested there was another reason I was excited to see her, my once best-friend-and-almost-girlfriend. But I tried not to think about that and focused on explaining everything to Lizzie.

"I left her a clue at the first place," I said, continuing my explanation. "I wrote NYC on the floor so she would know where we were headed."

"I saw you do that," Lizzie interrupted. "You got cut so you could leave a message."

"Yeah, I did," I continued. "Then, I wanted to continue the trail, and leave a clue in the next house. I saw that decoder in Nolly's pocket and stole it. I left it behind in the house. Meg must have found the clues. She probably figured out the decoder and how to use it. I've been thinking about that too. Remember when Cain said that there's some sort of secret message in Cain's dad's will? He said that it would take us on a scavenger hunt of sorts. I bet Meg somehow got access to the will and the decoder helped her figure out the scavenger hunt. That's how she knew to come here. After she got the decoder, she must have gotten a plane ride over here, and either stolen something that was supposed to be hidden here or left some kind of evidence that she had been here and that she's onto Cain. Cain probably figured out that someone had been here and then they figured out that the decoder was missing. That's why Cain is mad."

Lizzie just stared at me. I knew everything I said was a lot to take in. "Wow," she said. "I can't believe that you really are getting us out of here. All that stuff you did, that's crazy. Thank you."

I wasn't expecting that. I was expecting questions or doubts but not thanks. "You're welcome," I replied. "Trust me, I want to get out of here just as much as you do."

"If you need help with anything in your master escape plan in the future, just let me know," she replied. "Because I miss my family so much it hurts, and I'll do anything to get us home."

"I will," I replied, glad we were on the same team. "But if he asks us about stealing the decoder or leaving clues or anything, let me take the blame. You had nothing to do with it. Don't say a word. I don't want you to get hurt."

Lizzie looked at me. "I don't want you to take the fall by yourself," she replied. "Who knows what Cain will do to you . . ."

"Lizzie, no," I begged. "I don't want you getting hurt for something I did. Please just don't say anything or try to defend me. Please."

She looked at me for a while. "Fine," she said. "But, next time, you have to let me help you with your plan and you have to let me take the consequences with you."

"Deal," I said. "Here's my next plan. If my suspicions are right, Meg is already headed to the next stop on the scavenger hunt. We need to stall Cain to give her more time. We've got to keep them here as long as possible. Got any ideas?"

Before we could plan any further, Cain and Nolly came back into the room. He didn't waste any time getting down to the point. "Who stole the decoder? And you better fess up now because if you don't, you'll both be getting punished." My time to shine. "I did," I said, standing up, knowing that whatever was about to happen was not going to be pretty. Before I knew what was happening, the two henchmen grabbed me by the arms and dragged me into another room.

38

Meg

As soon as Kat sent me the decoded version of the will, I started on my way to Washington, D.C. According to the will, that was the next stop, and it was the second to last. Apparently, at the first place I stopped at in New York, Bill had left Cain a book of instructions on how to run the counterfeit scam. Cain had gotten the book from the first house, but the next stop was in Washington, D.C. and I was planning on getting there first and getting the key that Bill had left there.

Bill had said in the will that it was an "extra" key, so I assumed Cain had another key. Either way, I needed a key so I could get into the bunker. According to the will, the bunker was where all of Bill's printing presses were. It already had lots of counterfeit money and it had the means to make more. Finding this bunker and shutting it down was one of the main goals of my mission. I had to beat Cain to it, but first: the key.

I figured I was about one hour behind them, but, unlike Cain, I was able to take a plane. I had arranged with Kat earlier that morning for me to get a ride on one of the Keeper private jets. I had never flown before, so I was a little nervous. I also had no clue how an airport worked until my Keeper training. They really did cover all the details. Thanks to them, I knew exactly how to get on the private jet, but knowing how to do it and actually doing it were two different things.

Once I got to the airport and got through security, I got turned around a few times trying to find where to go. I eventually found the gate and boarded the plane. Since it was private and I was the only one who needed it at the moment, the plane took off as soon as I got there. I sat in my seat and stared out the window as the ground below me shrunk away. The people and buildings got smaller and smaller as the sky and clouds seemed to get bigger and bigger. We kept going up and the world kept shrinking.

Then, we broke through a layer of clouds and leveled out. It took my breath away. All around, all I could see was sky. There was a layer of clouds at my feet and a huge blue space above them. The sun was bright and reflecting off the clouds. It was stunning. Up here, it was easy to forget everything happening back down on Earth. It was so calm and simple. It was peaceful. For a second, I forgot about everything else but God's beautiful creation. But only for a second.

My phone buzzed, getting a notification. I glanced down and saw a reminder I had made a few months ago. "Order Mom's birthday gift." Her birthday was coming up. And I had completely forgotten. I looked out the window again, a tear sliding down my face. My mom had loved to travel. She would have loved to be on this plane with me right now. She had always wanted to fly to Europe. See the Eiffel tower, the Louvre, the Leaning Tower of Pisa, Big Ben.

We had never been able to afford any of it though because they were saving for my college. They always planned ahead, and they wanted me to be able to follow my dreams. And now they were gone, and my dreams of being a veterinarian had been all but forgotten. How did this all happen? How did I get so wrapped up in this Keeper stuff that I had forgotten what I loved to do?

Not only had I lost my parents, but I had lost who I was. I wasn't a tough, crime fighting, government agent. That was just who I had let them change me into. I was a shy, animal-loving, girl who wanted nothing more than to have her parents back. But if I couldn't have them back, I could at least do what they would have wanted me to do. And what they wanted me to do was definitely not what I was currently doing, traveling around the country in an attempt to stop a counterfeit scheme. They would have wanted me to go to college and become a vet. Follow my dreams. I was going to finish this case because I didn't quit what I started and my friends needed me, but after that, I was done. I was going to get my life back.

As the plane landed, my newfound determination and I got off the plane and into a rental car Kat had order for me. I followed the directions in the will and drove up to another shabby looking house. Again, using the will's directions, I went into the house and into one of the inner rooms. I picked one of the moldy books off of the decaying shelf and opened it, finding a maroon ribbon tied to a small key. Exactly what I was looking for.

I hurried back to my car, not knowing how far ahead of Cain I was and not wanting to run into him. As I drove off, I was thankful I hurried because when I stopped at the stop sign at the end of the street Bill's house was on, another car turned onto that street. Shooting a quick glance into the front seats, I saw Cain and one of his helpers. Thankfully, Cain didn't notice me, but it was a close call.

I sped up as I left the neighborhood, hoping to put as much distance between me and Cain as possible. After I got far enough away, I called Claudia, the IM (Individual Missions) Coordinator to fill her in. I had called Kat a few times and Kat had been passing information onto the IM, but I figured I should just relay the next phase of my plan to her directly. Plus, my plan was to ambush Cain at the bunker, and I would need a whole team to help me do that. The IM would be able to send the back-up I needed and to make sure that the whole operation went smoothly.

While I was talking to her, I also got her to set up another flight for me, this time to Jacksonville, Florida, the city noted in the bunker section of the will. I knew it would take Cain over a day to drive to Jacksonville since, again, he wouldn't be able to go by plane without the authorities recognizing him. I could go by plane, which would make the journey only two and a half hours. That would put me way ahead of him and give the team plenty of time to set up the ambush.

On my way to the airport, I called Kat. She would want to hear the most recent developments from me instead of the IM. Plus, I just wanted to talk to her. She was one of the only things keeping me going.

"Hello?" she said after the first ring. "Are you okay? How's the case? Do you need backup?"

"I'm fine, Kat. Calm down," I said, trying to reassure her. She let out a sigh of relief.

"Sorry, I was nervous. When you work in a business like this . . ."

"Sorry," I replied. "I get it. But I have good news!"

"You do??" Kat said excitedly. "I've heard general updates from higher up, but I want to hear it from you. Tell me all about the case!"

I then told her all about getting the key first but just barely. It felt good to tell a friend about everything. "Now I'm about to get on a plane that is heading to Florida. I called the IM and asked her to send backup to meet me there. I know that Cain is heading to his bunker where all the counterfeit money and equipment is held. I think we have about a day's lead on him. My plan is to set up an ambush at the bunker so we can catch him."

"Alright, I'll double check on dispatching back up right now," Kat replied, all business. "You know an ambush will be dangerous right?" she asked, sounding more concerned.

"I know," I responded. "But it's the only way to make sure we catch him so that this never happens again. I want to end this."

"Are you sure?" Kat asked. "If you give it more time, I'm sure we could figure something else out."

"I'm sure," I said. "If we wait, we might lose him, and I don't want him to be able to do anything like this ever again. Plus, I don't want Lizzie and Noah with him any longer than they have to be."

<h1 style="text-align:center">39</h1>

<h2 style="text-align:center">Lizzie</h2>

Noah was gone a really long time. I was nervous, like really nervous. I sat there on the floor of the decaying living room for what felt like forever. What were they doing to him? They wouldn't kill him, right? I was trying to convince myself. To be honest, I had no reason to believe that they wouldn't kill him or hurt him so bad he never recovered. These guys were ruthless.

I just couldn't believe Noah had done everything that he did. He had been working so hard to help us escape, and I hadn't even realized it. Even though I really hadn't had anything to do with his plans, I still somehow felt responsible for what was happening to him. Maybe because all the work he had done was helping me too and I felt like I needed to repay him? I wasn't sure, but either way I sat there worrying myself sick while across the room Nolly was sitting in an armchair texting on her phone. I guess since we all knew she wasn't a prisoner, there was no reason for her to have to live like one so Cain had given her phone back to her.

I watched her wondering what had happened to her, to us.

When had our friendship fallen apart so completely that she felt like betraying me and going behind my back like she had? And how could she sit there so nonchalantly while Noah was surely being tortured in the other room?

Suddenly, Nolly's phone dinged, telling her she got a text. She read it, then looked up, her eyes meeting mine. For a split second I thought I saw something of remorse on her face, but it was quickly replaced by a snide smirk.

"C'mon," she said, breaking me from my thoughts of her and my worry about Noah. "Follow me. Cain's orders." I got up and did what she said.

We went down a long hallway with peeling wallpaper and old, broken picture frames on the wall. One of the pictures caught my attention. It was a picture of what looked like a much younger Cain, probably four or five sitting on the knee of an older man who had similar features to Cain. I assumed it was his dad. He held a fishing pole and Cain was holding a miniature tackle box. He was smiling up at his dad and his dad was laughing at the camera.

I wondered what had happened to that. Cain used to be a smiling little boy without a care in the world and now he was a kidnapper who took pleasure in harming others. I looked around at some of the other pictures on the wall. The next picture over seemed to be from the same fishing trip. Cain still held his mini tackle box, but this time he was in the arms of a beautiful older woman. His mom. She had bright eyes, pretty smile wrinkles, and she looked at Cain like he hung the moon. She looked like the kind of person who made a room brighter just by being in it.

I looked at the wall for other pictures of her and saw her holding a baby Cain, holding hands with Cain's dad, posing with Cain on the first day of kindergarten, standing with Cain in a pumpkin patch, and posing for a family photo in front of the Christmas tree. Eventually though, she stopped appearing in the pictures. In all the pictures of Cain in middle school and high school, she wasn't there. Cain's smile wasn't as bright either.

That's when it hit me. She must have died. That's what happened to Cain. His mom, one of the brightest parts of his life, had died and his father and he hadn't known how to handle it. That's why they turned to crime. That's what happened to his smile.

"Lizzie?" Nolly said, calling my name from inside a room farther down the hallway. "You better hurry up and get in here."

I had been standing in the hallway, staring at the pictures for a hot second, so I quickly turned and walked down the hallway, still trying to process what I had learned about Cain's past. Part of me felt bad for him. The other part was telling me I was crazy because he had kidnapped me. I walked into the room where Nolly was to see her holding a length of rope.

"Nolly what are you doing?" I asked her, shocked that I was about to be tied up by my used to be best friend.

"Orders are orders," she said with a shrug, then proceeded to tie my hands behind my back and tie the rope to a hook on the wall. "You'll be sleeping here tonight," she said. "Don't try anything clever."

"How could you?" I asked her, tears starting to form in my eyes. I had been trying as hard as I could to be strong throughout this mess, but this was the final straw. "How could you do this?"

She stared at me. Her big blue eyes to my dull brown ones.

Then, "Honestly Lizzie, we haven't been close in a while. If you thought we were still friends, you were kidding yourself. When I was given the opportunity to gain power and wealth, of course I took it. It's nothing personal against you; you were just in the way."

And she turned around, left the room, and locked the door behind her. That's when the tears really came. I hadn't seen my family in forever and my ex-friend basically just told me I didn't mean anything to her, and I hadn't for a while. Not to mention that I had no idea what was happening to Noah, the only real friend I had here.

I cried until I had no tears left. Then I just stared at the wall in front of me, lost in my own thoughts. Eventually, I noticed that the room I was in was some kind of office/library. I started to read the titles of the books on the shelves across from me, trying to keep my brain from spiraling further. One title caught my eye. Not so much a title as a label. "Family Album."

Thankfully, the rope was long enough that I could get across the room and reach the book. I pulled it off the shelf and started flipping through the pages. I saw more pictures of little Cain and his mom and dad, back when they were together and happy. The pictures seemed like they spanned years and years, but at one point in the book, I turned the page, and it was blank. The rest of the book was too.

That must have been when Cain's mom died. She had been keeping up with the book, but when she died, no one wanted to keep it going. It was so sad. I couldn't imagine losing my mom like that. I would have started crying again, but I was too tired, so I closed the book, lay down, and tried to sleep.

My attempt to escape into blissful sleep was worthless though. I was too worried about Noah. No matter how hard I tried, my thoughts kept drifting to him, wondering if he was okay. I didn't have to wonder much longer though because Noah was thrown into the room minutes later. They didn't tie him up, but clearly there was no need to.

His face was black and blue, and his clothes were bloody. His right eye was swollen shut and his nose was bleeding. "Noah," I whispered, concerned and shocked, scooting over to him.

"Dinner," a gruff voice said passing in two plates, napkins, and cups.

I used some of our dinner supplies to clean up Noah. I used the water and napkins to clean the blood off his face. I put the stew, which was cold, in the cup and held it to Noah's mouth, trying to get him to eat something. When he wouldn't, I helped him lie down, and I covered him up with my jacket. He hadn't even said anything. Thankfully, he was alive, but he was in bad shape.

I was just so sick and tired of these people. How could they do this to us? All I could do though was pray that Meg had some sort of amazing plan to save us before it was too late. I lay down and tried again to fall asleep but ended up staying awake the rest of the night worrying about Noah. He had become my friend over the past few days, and I was terrified I would lose him. These people weren't messing around. I had no doubt that they wouldn't hesitate to kill us if we messed up again.

40

Nolly

That night, Cain called me and his two cronies (who he really should just get rid of because they literally don't do anything) into his office. It was another one of those gross, decaying rooms with peeling paint and rat poop on the floor. There was an old desk in the middle with two chairs in front of it. The chairs were kind of falling apart, so we all just stood behind them.

"So, as you already know, those little brats gave away our information. I'm assuming there will be people at the bunker waiting for us, so here's my plan."

Woah, wait what? People waiting at the bunker? To catch us? This was a disaster. When this had all first started, I had just kind of assumed that Cain was good enough that we wouldn't get caught. I had never really considered what would happen if we did. Until now. I loved helping Cain and continuing my parents' legacy, but I did not want to go to prison. Wearing an orange jumpsuit every day? Yuck. Plus, I heard that the food in prison is awful. While I was starting to inwardly panic, Cain continued telling us the plan.

"Huxley and Harrison one of you will go in disguised as me and pretend to be me. The other will try to get in undetected. When they try to take the fake me, put up a fight. Make it messy. Draw them all in and get rid of as many of them as possible. Meanwhile, I'll be going in using the back entrance. Most of them should have been drawn away from there by that point, but if not, I'll have a gun on me. I will use the back entrance to go in and grab as much cash as I can. While I'm doing that, Nolly will take the kids out of the car and dump them at the side of the building. Then, we'll escape."

That was a lot. A lot of getting rid of people and a lot of guns. I was all in for making fake money and getting rich, but killing people? That was a different story. Was I ready for that level of crime? It didn't seem like Cain was really going to give me an option.

That wasn't the only part of his plan that I didn't like. Why was he only grabbing cash? That was going to run out pretty fast. Was it really worth it to go through all of this for just some cash? He probably had a deeper plan because he didn't seem like the kind of guy to risk getting caught for anything less than a million dollars. I just had to wait and hope he let me in on that part of the plan.

Another thing didn't add up either. The kids. Why were we leaving them behind? "Why don't we take them with us," I asked Cain, wondering why he would just let them go. They had so much dirt on us, it made me nervous to just give them up like that.

"It will give the authorities less incentive to follow us," Cain replied. "They'll have my bunker and the kids, so while they will still be after me, it may not be as heavily as before. Plus, the kids already ruined one plan. I don't need them ruining another."

That felt pointed at me. When he said the kids, he wasn't including me right? Because it really wasn't my fault they found out. Or at least that's what I was trying to convince myself. He even said it himself that he was part of the problem, calling me out to talk to him.

Thinking back, that was really stupid of us. It was so easy for them to figure it out, and then the whole plan was ruined. Now I'm going to have to deal with all these agent people dying. I didn't want to see any of that or even be in the area when all that went down.

I wish at the beginning of everything Cain had told me all that was involved. I guess he didn't know that it would come down to this, but he had to have some idea something like this could happen. He should have warned me. And now, after hearing that comment about the kids ruining everything, I was worried he was mad at me and was going to leave me behind in the aftermath of all that bloodshed. I had to make absolutely sure that that was not going to happen.

"Does everyone understand the plan?" Cain asked, drawing me out of my thoughts. We all nodded. "Good. We leave at dawn," Cain said, dismissing us. Huxley and Harrison left the room, but I went over and sat in the decaying chair right in front of Cain.

Thankfully, the chair held me up because this was important, and I needed to be sure I got my point across. "Yes, Nolly?" Cain asked with a smirk. I decided to just be blunt.

"You know very well that the chances of Huxley and Harrison leaving the bunker are not very high." He nodded. "But my chances of leaving the bunker alive are much better." Again, he nodded. "So, if you even think about leaving the bunker without me, you better think again." I tried glaring at him with as much force possible, but I think I just looked like a toddler trying to boss around her babysitter. And Cain's response said he saw me as just that.

"Yes, Ma'am," he said, his smile getting bigger. This was so annoying. He clearly didn't take me seriously.

"You care to tell me why we are risking our lives for a relatively small amount of fake money? You going to tell me your real plan here?"

"Nope," he said with a laugh. "My plans are private from now on in case the walls are listening." He laughed again.

Clearly, all this stress was making him go crazy. Not seeing what was so amusing about the life-or-death situation that was quickly approaching, I got up and left. If he was going to be sassy and weird towards me, I sure as heck could be sassy right back. I walked down the hall to a bedroom that I was supposed to be staying in. Like all the other rooms in this house and in all the houses we had been in, the room looked like it was rotting. It smelled like it too.

Suddenly, I felt claustrophobic. I needed out. This was too much. I turned around and walked as fast as I could towards the back door, trying to not make any noise. The last thing I needed right now was to run into Cain or one of his cronies. I yanked the back door open, stepping out into the cold night air. I walked away from the house for a little bit, trying to calm down my racing thoughts and fast breathing.

I found a small tree stump and sat down, cradling my head in my hands. This was going all wrong. I was expecting this to be a grand adventure. I was supposed to be Cain's right-hand girl, not his failure double agent. I was supposed to become rich, not sleep in falling apart houses every night. I was supposed to be having the thrill of a lifetime following in my parents' footsteps, not sitting here wondering if I would be alive at this time tomorrow. For the first time since everything started, I wondered if I had made the right decision. Hopefully, what I was doing would get my parents' attention and make them proud of me, but at what cost?

I sat on the stump for a while, just staring at nothing and worrying myself sick. Eventually I pulled out my phone to check the time. It was well past midnight. I knew I needed to go inside and go to bed, but I felt frozen.

Suddenly I heard footsteps behind me. I turned my head in time for someone to grab my arm and roughly pull me up, grab my phone out of my hand and drag me back towards the house. After I got over my disorientation, I realized it was Cain.

"Cain, what are you doing?" I asked him, startled.

"I should ask you the same thing," he growled, not even looking at me.

"I was just sitting outside getting some fresh air," I said, still confused. Why was he so upset?

"Yeah, right," he said with a dark chuckle. He walked me the rest of the way to my room in silence. When we got there, he pushed me past the doorway and I turned around to look at him, hoping for an explanation.

"If you are doing anything at all to double-cross me, I can get rid of you like that," he said, snapping his fingers.

"Cain, no that's not-," I started, but didn't get to finish because he slammed the door. Then, I heard the lock turn. He had just locked me in. He had taken my phone back and locked me in a room.

For some reason, he had stopped trusting me. Maybe it was because of Noah and Lizzie realizing I was a traitor or because he was getting paranoid now. Maybe he thought I was trying to escape? Or maybe he thought I was using my phone to call someone? Either way, our partnership was over.

Without anything else to do, I climbed into the bed in the center of the room and covered up with the moth-eaten blankets, hoping to drift off to sleep so I didn't have to think about what just happened and how much it scared me. I tossed and turned all night.

The next morning, as we all got in the car, I tried to catch Cain's eye, but he wouldn't look at me. The car ride was long, painfully so. I sat there in silence, trying to avoid my worried thoughts. Eventually, I was able to drift off and catch up on some of the sleep I had lost the night before.

I woke up right when we passed a sign announcing we were in Florida. When we finally pulled up to the bunker, I was nervous for about a million reasons. If we got caught or worse killed . . . I didn't even want to think about it.

41

Meg

We were all set up. There were 18 of us. I knew that it was a lot, but we had to make sure we caught these guys. We just had to. We had been prepping and planning for the past day.

When I saw Cain's car in DC, I called in the plate number, and one of the teams back at the Keeper HQ was using traffic cameras to track him, so thankfully we were able to get a pretty good estimate of when he would arrive.

As soon as I had told the IM Coordinator that I was headed to the bunker, the planning had started. They had gotten a team together, briefed them, and had them on a plane to Florida within the hour. I had spent almost my entire plane ride on the phone with different people, talking about details of the plan.

Once we all arrived, we started by scouting out the bunker, making sure we understood all the ins and outs and checking for booby traps. Thankfully, there were none, and I was glad I had the other agents helping me because I would probably not have thought to check for them.

We spent the remainder of the time finalizing the plan and

making sure everyone understood their assignments. I would be at the back entrance, which we found when scouting out the bunker, with three of the other agents. When they arrived, I would sneak around and get the kids out of the car. Another agent would follow me to help cover me and make sure we got the kids to safety. The rest of the agents would either be guarding the entrance or hiding in the bunker, making sure no one escaped.

There was a nervous energy throughout the bunker. We all knew what was about to happen. I think some of us also suspected that not all of us would make it out alive. We weren't entirely sure how far Cain would go. He might cave easily, but I doubted it. A bad shootout was a more likely possibility.

I just couldn't believe this was happening. A few short months ago I was starting out my completely normal and honestly boring senior year and now I was living out a spy movie. And not the good kind of spy movie. The kind that you barely even want to watch because it's so stressful. My main priority was to save the kids. Then, I would be able to go back to a normal life, or as normal a life as it could be after all of this.

I was just so nervous, but nervous wasn't even a good enough word. I felt like I was going to cry, throw up, and pass out all at once. I wasn't even sure if that was possible, but if it was, I was about to do it. "Take a deep breath, Meg," I whispered to myself. "You got this." I had to do this. I had to save the kids.

It was crazy to me that I was referring to them as kids in my head when I was the same age as them, but I felt so much older. Something about being a spy in charge of people's lives does that to a person, I guess. I didn't even know what I was going to do if one of them didn't make it, but I couldn't think like that. I had to trust that we would all make it out of this alive.

Suddenly, I heard car doors slamming. Someone yelled "They're here!" And everything became still. From my position in the back, I could see a shadow of a person come in through the front entrance and raise his arm. A second later, a gunshot fired. A second after that, multiple more shots were fired, and the commotion had begun.

That was my cue. This was going to be messy, and people were going to die. As much as that made me what to sink to the floor in a little ball and cry, I had to stay strong and do my job. I snuck out the back entrance with another agent right behind me. My gun was out, and I was prepared to shoot even though I was really hoping I wouldn't have to. My plan was to shoot to injure, not kill. I just couldn't bring myself to do that, even for my own protection.

We rounded the corner, running at full speed, and I came face to face with Cain. This had happened in my nightmares more times than I would care to admit, and now it was happening in real life. He had a gun pulled out and ready to fire, and we both fired at the exact same time. My bullet landed in Cain's arm, a testament to good training because it felt like my brain was completely frozen. I looked down at my body, half expecting to see a bullet wound.

When I realized I was fine, I turned to make sure my partner was okay. He was on the ground. Cain's bullet had landed in his chest. I bent down towards the agent without even thinking about what I was doing, tears starting to form in my eyes. He was gone. That could have just as easily been me. My brain was not working at all. I heard yelling in the background, but I couldn't register what the person was saying. This was too much. There was so much blood. I stared at the bullet hole in my partner's chest for a second before I remembered what I was doing. I sprang to my feet, turning back around just in time to see Cain pulling his fist back. Then everything else around me faded to black.

42

Lizzie

This is bad. This is bad. This is so, so bad. That was all that was running through my head, as Noah and I sat huddled together next to the bunker. When we had pulled up earlier, Cain and the two kidnapper dudes had gotten out of the car and headed towards the small metal building. Nolly got out too after telling Noah and me to stay put, and she went around to the back of the car and opened up the trunk. She pulled out rope and fabric then came back towards Noah and me. She was going to tie us up. Again. I was so sick of this.

She opened the car door and motioned for me to come closer to her. For a second, I considered running. Nolly would be so easy to overpower and Noah and I could finally escape. But then I thought about what would happen to Nolly if we did. She would probably get in so much trouble with Cain if we escaped while she was in charge of us. I knew that she had betrayed us so I should have no desire to protect her or help her in any way, but I still didn't want her to get hurt. And if I was being really honest, I still thought that the old Nolly, the one who was fun and sweet and silly and outgoing, was still in there, and maybe one day, she would realize where she went wrong, and we could be friends again. It would take a very long time to rebuild our trust, if that was even possible, but some part of me hoped it was.

So, I didn't run. Which turned out to be a very good thing because a few seconds later Cain came up behind Nolly. "Listen to her and do what she says," Cain growled. "Or I won't hesitate to use this," he said, pulling out a gun and pointing it at Noah and me. I took a sharp breath in and stayed absolutely still until Cain lowered the gun.

"Better be quick," he said to Nolly. "It's going to be nasty. There are lots of people in there." Then he walked away.

Lots of people in the bunker? I thought as Nolly started to tie my hands together. Noah was right then. Meg and, I guess, other agents had gotten here before us. I assumed they were probably trying to get us back and capture Cain. My worry instantly grew. Cain was ruthless and people would probably die.

All I wanted was to be saved, but not at this cost. I wanted to run in the bunker and warn everyone, but since that wasn't really an option I just prayed. As Nolly finished tying me up, I tried to catch her eye, but she wouldn't look at me.

"You don't have to do this, you know," I said to her.

"You don't get it," she said, moving on to tying up Noah.

"What do you mean?" I asked. She looked miserable. Was Cain somehow forcing her to do this? For a minute, she didn't say anything, and I thought she was going to ignore me.

But eventually she said, "This is what my parents do. This crime stuff. All my life, they've barely given me the time of day. They never talk to me, and they don't even know the first thing about me. I thought that if I helped Cain, I would get to follow in their footsteps and impress them. Maybe they would finally see me."

In that moment, I felt so bad for her. She had been so caught up in seeking her parents' approval that nothing else mattered to her. She was trying to gain the love and acceptance of people who didn't even pay attention to her. All her life she had failed, and she was hoping that this was her opportunity.

"Nolly, I-"

"No, Lizzie. Just stop. This might still work out. Just please be quiet and let me do what I have to do."

"But Nolly-,"

"Just stop talking. Please."

So, I did. This was terrible. I had thought Noah and I were trapped, but turns out, Nolly had been trapped too. While Noah and I were chained physically, Nolly was chained emotionally, constantly trying to impress her parents.

We sat in silence while Nolly finished tying us up. She motioned for us to follow her, and I climbed out of the car, then turned to help Noah out. He hadn't said much during the car ride, partly because he had slept the whole time. He was in really bad shape, and it looked like he was in pain every time he moved. We followed Nolly to the side of the bunker.

"Sit here," she said. "Stay here until we are gone."

"Wait, you're leaving us here?" I asked, stunned. After all we had been through, they were just going to let us go?

"Yes," Nolly said. "Cain thinks if we don't take you with us, they won't want to catch us as badly." Then she turned and started walking away.

"Wait, Nolly!" I called out. "Where are you and Cain going? How are you getting away?" What was their plan? I didn't want Nolly to go anywhere else with Cain, and I didn't really think that they were going to be able to escape all the agents at the bunker.

I could hear the sound of gunshots echoing through the bunker now as I sat there trying to understand everything that was going on and trying to take a guess at Cain's plan.

I leaned over to Noah, about to ask him what he thought of it all when we saw Meg round the corner on our right and Cain round the corner on our left. They were headed straight at each other, and they both had their guns out. Noah started freaking out next to me and trying to stand up.

"Help me, Lizzie," he grunted. I realized that he was trying to help Meg, and I desperately wanted to help her too. I tried to help Noah up, but my hands were still tied.

"I don't know what to do, Noah," I said, starting to panic. Meg had been the one to save us and I did not want to watch her die. There was nothing we could do though. They both fired at the same time. We saw the guard behind her fall, and Meg turned around and bent down towards him. Cain was walking up behind her, looking like he was about to hurt her.

"MEG!" Noah screamed. "Meg, get up!" Cain turned and fired a bullet in our direction, hitting the wall just to the right of Noah. Then Cain reached Meg and knocked her out. Noah kept screaming as Cain dragged Meg over to the car. I was trying to get out of my ropes, hoping to be able to help her, but it wasn't working. Cain put her in the backseat and drove away. Noah just stared after the car.

I wasn't sure what Cain was going to do with her, but I was worried, to say the least. Cain was ruthless. She had helped us become free, and now I felt like it was our job to do the same for her. I was prepared to do whatever I had to do to help her. The look in Noah's eyes told me he felt the same way.

All around us there was the sound of crashing and gunfire. I grabbed a sharp piece of debris from nearby and started hacking at my ropes. I cut through it pretty quickly and began to cut Noah lose. As soon as we were free, I helped Noah up and we started walking away from the building. We had to come up with a plan and we couldn't do that if we were trying to keep from getting shot.

"What should we do?" I asked Noah, having no clue where to even start.

"Honestly," Noah started but was interrupted by a huge fireball exploding behind us, sending the entire bunker up in flames and pushing us off the ground and away from where we were last standing. A bomb. There were not only guns, but bombs and now every agent that was inside fighting the bad guys, everyone that was able to help us, everyone who we would have told about Meg was probably dead.

Noah and I were sprawled out on the ground way out in front of the bunker. My ears were ringing, my head was spinning, and I felt nauseous. I rolled over onto my stomach and threw up in the grass. I lay back down and waited for the mess that was in my head to go away. After a solid ten minutes, I was able to sit up.

I hadn't been hurt too badly except for a large gash on my leg. I looked over at Noah, who was also sitting up, which I took to be a good sign. He looked no worse than he had before the bomb, which really wasn't saying much. I think he was running off pure adrenaline at this point because he looked terrible.

"What on earth are we supposed to do now?" I asked.

"Either we go search the bunker for anything that could help, or we start walking and hope there's a town around here somewhere where we can get help." Taking one look at Noah, I knew he would not survive anything longer than a ten-minute walk.

"Let's check the bunker first," I suggested. We pulled ourselves up off the ground and carefully walked back to the bunker. The kidnapper and other guy who was helping Cain were laying just inside the door. Dead. They must have set the bomb off, then tried to escape. They just weren't fast enough. I almost threw up again.

We went inside and looked around. There was blood and ashes everywhere. We picked through the rubble and found body after body. No one was alive. By the time we walked back outside having no clue what to do, I was crying. So many people were gone. We had to help Meg but didn't know how. We didn't find anything helpful in the bunker and I had no idea how far away the next town was.

Suddenly, we saw a car coming towards us. Cain's car. Noah grabbed weapons, guns from some of the dead agents, and we ran back into the building.

43

Nolly

"What's going on?" I asked Cain. "I thought you were getting money, not her," I said referring to the agent girl he had just thrown into the backseat. I had gone back and waited in the car after I had dropped off Lizzie and Noah. I was just sitting there waiting when Cain suddenly threw open the back door and threw an unconscious government agent into the seat.

"Oh, trust me, she's worth much more than money. She's worth freedom," he replied, as he climbed into the driver's seat and started the car.

"What do you mean?" I asked, still confused. I knew our partnership was over, but this was a pretty important detail to not tell me.

"We are going to get her to call into her agency and tell them that everyone died in the explosion and that it was too much for her to handle, so she's quitting her job. That way they won't look for us anymore. Then, we'll kill her."

"What explosion?" I asked. Just then, it sounded like a bomb went off behind us. A big plume of smoke flowed into the sky.

"That explosion," Cain said, smirking. "I gave Huxley a bomb to set off to kill everyone in there." He was telling me all of this like our conversation the previous night hadn't happened. Like he didn't think I was going to double-cross him. I was so lost. Was he mad at me or not? Were we partners or not? I was getting so tired of trying to keep up with him. Tired of trying to please my parents. Tired of this whole thing. But there was nothing I could do about it now. It wasn't like I could go back to my old life without spending some serious time in prison first.

Suddenly, we made a U-turn. "Where are we going?" I asked.

"Back to the bunker. There's another secret to it. Half of it is underground. We are going back to get all the money and kill the girl. Then, we'll leave."

Kill the girl. That was not something I wanted to be a part of. I didn't want to be part of any of this anymore. I had let my desire for approval and attention consume me and now I was trapped in this awful life of crime. I didn't know what to do. It felt like there was nothing I could do. We reached the bunker and got out of the car.

"C'mon, help me carry her," Cain said, motioning to the unconscious agent.

"Um, I'll just wait here for you, you know, watch the car," I replied.

"Help. Me. Carry. Her," Cain said fiercely, the anger I had seen in his eyes last night coming back full force.

I walked over to the side of the car and helped Cain get her out. We carried the girl through the ruins towards the back of the bunker. I was getting creeped out walking through the bomb site. I felt like we were being watched. I stayed silent though, trying to avoid any more of Cain's anger.

Cain leaned down and opened a metal trap door in the floor, and we carried the agent down into the secret area. There was a desk with chairs around it in front of a big machine that I assumed printed the money. The rest of the room was covered in counterfeit money. Piles and piles of it. There was so much. The room was also pretty smokey, so Cain left the hatch to the secret entrance open to let it air out. We sat the agent down in a chair, and Cain tied her to it.

"Here," he said, tossing me a canvas bag he had picked up from a pile on the floor. "Fill this up, then start on another." I did as I was told and began stuffing the bag with fake money while Cain watched the agent girl come to.

"So, " Cain said, when the girl was finally awake. "You are going to call your agency and tell them I'm dead, or else I'll make sure your death is very painful."

"No," the girl said. "You can torture me all you want, but you will be found one day, and you will pay for your crimes." Wow. She was crazy. Or just really brave. Even in the face of a painful death, she stood for what was right.

In that moment, I wished I was more like her. I wished that on that day when Cain had picked me up in his car that I had said no. I wished that I had stood up for what's right. And most of all, I wished I had never stopped being friends with Lizzie. She was the most positive influence in my life, and I had pushed her away.

Maybe if I had listened to her more instead of brushing her off and calling her a goody-two-shoes, I wouldn't be in this situation. Maybe if we had stayed friends, I would have learned from her and I would have known how to say no to Cain instead of just going along with what he wanted. Maybe if I had accepted that our friendship and her love for me was enough, I wouldn't have felt the need to gain attention from my parents.

Suddenly, I heard a sound from above me. I looked up and thought I saw Lizzie's face peeking over the edge of the hole for the trap door. I shook it off and got back to shoving money in the bag, thinking I had to have imagined it.

"Give up, Cain," the agent said. "You won't win this." Cain then drew out a knife and prepared to throw it at her, but before he could, another knife thrown from the shadowy ceiling lodged in his arm.

44

Noah

We had hidden in the building behind a pile of debris and waited to see what Cain was going to do. We didn't really have a plan, and I honestly wasn't sure if I was going to be able to do anything useful. It hurt my entire body to move. I was bruised from head to toe and even breathing hurt. But I wasn't going to let Cain escape and get away with everything he had done, and I definitely wasn't going to let him hurt Meg. Not without a fight.

I didn't really understand all my feelings towards her, but I did know that I had to protect her, especially after all she had done to help us. Cain and Nolly walked past Lizzie and me, carrying Meg in between them. I froze. What if Meg was already . . .? No, I couldn't think like that. I stared at her as they passed, trying to see any sign that she was still alive. Then I saw her chest rise and fall, just the slightest amount. She was breathing. That was a good sign.

My relief was instantly replaced with anger. Hot, fiery anger. Anger that Cain had hurt Meg as much as he did. Anger that Cain had hurt me as much as he did. Thankfully, Lizzie was fine physically, but emotionally? We were all scarred.

Suddenly, a piece of rubble fell from the ceiling and hit my back, sending a wave of pain through me. It wasn't a big piece of rubble, but it had landed right on a wound from the night before. Lizzie noticed my grimace and looked at me with a worried expression asking me with her face if I was okay. I nodded, trying to focus on my anger and my desire to bring Cain to justice instead of all the pain.

I watched Cain open a hatch in the floor and carry Meg down below. Nolly also disappeared into the underground bunker, and I motioned to Lizzie that we should follow them. We walked slowly through the bunker, trying to stay as silent as possible. Lizzie noticed something a little off to our right and motioned for me to pause so she could go check it out.

I waited, getting antsy and hating the idea of Meg down there with Cain. Lizzie came back and showed me three knives that were a little battered, but still in decent shape. She handed me two of them and we kept walking towards the trap door. Now I had two knives and a gun I had found earlier. It made me feel better to know I had a way of protecting myself and fighting back, but I still wasn't sure how all of this was going to go down.

When we got to the opened trap door, we bent down next to it, trying to hear what they were saying. I knew we couldn't just climb down there, so I wasn't really sure what to do. I could make out enough to hear that Cain was threatening Meg and I got my knife ready, not wanting to use it but knowing that I would if it looked like Cain was going to try to hurt Meg.

Meg said something to Cain that I couldn't quite make out, but apparently, Cain didn't like it very much because he pulled out a knife of his own. My anger from earlier returned full force, and I knew I had to do something to protect her. I threw the knife. It landed in Cain's arm. Cain let out an angry roar, looking around for where the knife came from.

I dropped down from the ceiling, landing not-so-gracefully on the ground. At least I was on my feet. My adrenaline had completely taken over, and all my pain from earlier was gone. I looked up and realized Cain was advancing towards me. And he had pulled out a gun. I threw my other knife, this one landing in his leg. I then grabbed my gun while Lizzie was working on untying Meg. I hadn't seen her come in from the ceiling, but I was glad she had. I wasn't alone in fighting.

Cain and I both aimed our guns at each other, but we didn't fire. We knew that if one of us did, the other would too. Cain threw a knife, but I dodged it. We circled around each other for a few seconds. Out of the corner of my eye I saw Lizzie had finished untying Meg, and they were standing behind Cain. Lizzie had given Meg her knife and Meg was taking aim. The way Cain and I were walking around each other didn't give her a clear shot though. If she missed by the slightest bit, she might hit me. I could tell that's what she was thinking.

I could also see something else in her dark brown eyes. Something like remorse. She wasn't the kind of person that wanted to hurt someone else, no matter how much they had done to deserve it. Cain and I kept circling each other, getting closer and closer. We were about two feet away from each other when he suddenly ran at me, pulling out another knife. I tried to get out of the way, but I wasn't fast enough, and he stabbed my right arm. It felt like it was on fire. Blood was pouring from a deep hole, but I didn't have time to be hurt.

I whirled around and fired my gun in his direction, missing badly and putting a hole in a stack of money, sending little paper shreds everywhere. Cain fired his gun, but I think because of all the paper shreds flying through the air he couldn't see because it hit another stack of money far to my left.

Eventually the paper cleared, and we were back to circling. I wasn't sure how much longer I would make it. I was starting to get lightheaded from all the blood I was losing from my arm.

"Give it up, Noah," Cain growled.

"No, Cain. You give it up. I'm not going to let you hurt me or Meg or Lizzie any more than you already have."

"Aww, well, isn't that sweet," he said, getting closer and closer to me. We continued circling each other in silence as I started feeling weaker and weaker. I was pretty sure he knew what was going on and was just waiting for me to pass out. I was slowing down, and my movements were getting sluggish. It was getting hard to breath.

"Getting a little sleepy there, Noah?" Cain taunted.

"This isn't over, Cain. You will have to pay. Good will always win over evil. Maybe not today, but it will. Just you wait."

Getting too weak to stand, I collapsed on the floor. Cain walked towards me and aimed his gun at my chest. Just when I thought he would shoot, a voice called out, "Drop your weapons," and people came storming down the stairs. I knew it must have been more back up agents, but everything was starting to get so blurry I couldn't really see them. Some part of my brain processed that help had come and that I really might make it out of here alive. But then, I heard a final gunshot. I saw a still smoking gun in Cain's hand. I looked down and saw red blooming from my stomach and passed out.

45

Lizzie

He shot Noah. That crazy, awful lunatic shot Noah. Once that shot rang out, everything in the bunker descended into pure chaos. Agents were trying to get to Cain to stop him and catch him, but he had absolutely lost it. He was shooting at anyone who came near him. Shreds of paper were flying through the air and the room was filling with gun smoke.

For the past couple of minutes, Nolly had been sitting in the corner, hugging her knees to her chest and watching everything go down with wide, tear-filled eyes. I could see by the look on her face she had realized that she had gotten herself into a big mess and she wanted nothing more than to escape. Through the haze of smoke, I saw Nolly get off the ground and slowly make her way over to Cain. She grabbed his arm and pulled him off to the side. For a moment, everything went quiet. Cain had stopped shooting, and so had the agents.

"Cain," Nolly said just above a whisper, but it rang out through the room. "Let's escape while we can. If we run now, they might not chase us." I wasn't sure if she thought escape was actually possible or if she was just trying to calm Cain down. She looked so scared.

"Cain, please," she begged, tugging on his arm that wasn't holding the gun. The agents just stood there, unsure of what to do. We were all quiet as we waited for Cain's response.

He turned to Nolly and yelled, "Nolly, don't you get it?? This is it! We aren't going to make it out of this. They are going to kill us, and if they don't, we will spend the rest of our lives rotting in prison! It's all your fault for not keeping a closer watch on the kids. If you had not gotten that stupid decoder stolen right out from under you, we wouldn't be in this situation." He paused, turning to look at her more closely, like he was realizing something. "It's all your fault," he whispered softly, looking at her menacingly.

Nolly started to back away from him. "No, Cain, no," she said, starting to cry. "It's not my fault. I'm sorry. You said you didn't blame me for that."

He raised his gun. "Well people lie, don't they? Have you been lying to me too? You haven't been fully committed lately. I haven't been able to trust you. You were trying to get me caught, weren't you?" Cain was getting closer and closer to her.

"No, Cain, no! I promise!" Nolly said frantically, backing away. "I didn't do anything to try to mess all this up. Ever since the beginning all I've done was try to impress you and make my parents proud. I promise I didn't betray you. Please . . . please don't hurt me."

But Cain wasn't listening. He was going to shoot her, I knew it. He cocked the gun. It was at that moment I knew I had to stop him. Even if Nolly had betrayed my trust and our friendship, I still loved her. I would give up anything to save her, even if it meant giving up my own life. I was too far away from Cain to get the gun from him, but I was close enough to Nolly to push her out of the way.

I started running towards her and it felt like time slowed down. Meg tried to hold me back, but I brushed her off. She didn't understand how much I loved Nolly and why I had to do this. Cain pulled the trigger right as I shoved Nolly to the ground, knowing that I would get the bullet instead. Nolly and I both fell, and she looked at the red spot growing on my chest. Right on my heart. While the rest of the world fell into chaos around us, all I could see was her.

"Lizzie," she cried, tears streaming down her face. "Why did you do that? I didn't deserve that. I've been terrible to you." Nolly was sobbing now.

"I love you, Nolly," I said gasping for air. "You've always been my friend, and I couldn't let him do that to you."

"I don't know what to say. I'm so, so sorry for betraying you. I–"

I cut her off. "I forgive you, Nolly."

"You forgive me? But I don't deserve it."

"I know," I replied. "But I forgive you anyway." She sat there, holding my hand and crying, then Meg was at my side.

"Lizzie . . ." she gasped, staring at me.

"Meg," I said, struggling to get the words out. "Will you do something for me?"

"Anything," she replied, tears starting to fall down her face.

"Promise me that you'll do everything in your power to make sure they go easy on Nolly. I want her to be able to have a new life, not one spent in prison."

"I'll try, Lizzie," Meg responded, sounding unsure. "I'm just not sure if I can do anything about that."

"Just promise me you'll do everything you can."

"I–I promise," she said, tears sliding down her face. I nodded in thanks, suddenly finding it really hard to talk. Meg and Nolly sat next to me, holding my hands and crying as the world slowly faded away to black.

46

Meg

Lizzie was asleep. That's all it was. She was just tired and taking a nap. She was fine. That's what I was trying to convince myself of as I sat crying on the floor holding Lizzie's hand. All around me, the world was falling apart. There was smoke and flying bits of counterfeit money filling the air, making it difficult to see very far in front of me. I didn't know what to do. It was like all my training had suddenly left my brain. All I could think about was Lizzie. And Noah. He had been shot in the stomach and had already lost so much blood, all because he was trying to protect Lizzie and me.

I had been so confused about how I felt about Noah, and I had just been brushing it off, trying to focus on saving him and Lizzie, but now I knew that I wanted to get to know him again. I wanted another chance at the relationship we never had. But now that might not happen. He might already be gone, and I would never get to talk to him again, never get to thank him for all that he had done to help me find them, never get to thank him for jumping in and saving my life.

My tears were falling harder now. I was so, so scared I would never get to see him again. I had known all along that Cain was evil and ruthless, but I never thought it would get this bad.

People were shouting all around me, moving around in colorful blurs. The back-up agents tried to get the gun from Cain, but they couldn't. I don't know if Cain's gun was able to hold a massive number of bullets or if he had switched guns at some point, but either way he would fire anytime someone got near him, and he hadn't been without a bullet yet. The agents were trying to take him alive and not shoot as much, but they had to abandon that plan with the way Cain was shooting. It ended up being a total shootout.

I knew I needed to help, but I could barely move. My body was frozen. It was like I was split into two different people: the old version of me who just wanted to go home, curl into her parents' arms, and cry herself to sleep and the agent version of me who knew she needed to do something to help if she even wanted her friends to have the slightest chance of living.

Right now, I wasn't sure who I was anymore. I wasn't who I used to be, not anymore after all of this, but I also wasn't the hard-core agent they had trained me to be. I was somewhere in between. And I was frozen. I listened to the gunfire around me and sobbed even harder. I couldn't help. People were around me, dying, and there was nothing I could do about it. I had no weapon, and even if I did, I knew I wouldn't be able to use it to hurt anyone. I sat there, helplessly, waiting.

Then, all of a sudden, it became quiet. The gunfire stopped. I couldn't see anyone moving through the haze. Everything was still and silent until, "We got him," an agent said. They got him. They got Cain. It was finally, absolutely, without a doubt, over. I was done. I was done being an agent. My job was over. The bad guy was dead.

I started crying even harder now, the relief of being done washed over me and the heaviness of the day overwhelmed me. Medical agents came running down the stairs with stretchers. They quickly took an assessment of everyone's wounds and got to work. They put Noah and Lizzie each on a stretcher and carried them out of the bunker into the daylight. I was still sitting on the floor, silent tears pouring down my face, my head throbbing. I knew I needed to get up and start helping those who were wounded, but my body wouldn't move. Eventually, an agent came over to me.

"Meg, how are you? Do you need help?"

"I–I don't know," I said honestly. Emotionally, I was a tangled mess of worry, relief, confusion, sadness, and a thousand other emotions. Physically? I figured I should be good enough to walk myself out of the bunker. If only my body would listen to my brain and actually move.

"Help me stand?" I asked the agent, not trusting myself to do it on my own. The agent reached out his hand to pull me up, but as I started to stand, I got really dizzy and started to fall. Thankfully, the agent caught me before I hit the ground.

"Meg, I think you may need someone to carry you out," the agent said gently.

"I did get knocked out earlier," I said, remembering now why my head hurt so badly. It had been the longest of long days and I was having a hard time keeping everything straight in my head.

"Okay, you just wait here, Meg. I'll be right back." The agent walked away. She really was nice. What was her name again?

All the smoke had cleared from the room, but pieces of paper were still floating around and falling to the ground like snow. In fact, the entire floor of the room was covered in a layer of shredded fake money, making it look like a green-tinted snowbank. If only I was out in the snow, building a snow fort and preparing to have a snowball fight with my dad. Waiting for my mom to call us in for cocoa. If only.

I started crying again, remembering how this all started. Even though this mission was over, I still didn't have my parents to go home to. I wanted to keep crying, but it was as if I ran out of tears. The room had almost emptied around me. All of the injured had been evacuated. Someone had cuffed Nolly and taken her up.

I would keep my promise to Lizzie and make sure Nolly was taken care of and that the people in charge realized how much Nolly not spending the rest of her life in jail meant to Lizzie. I was still holding on to a faint hope that Lizzie would make it to tell them herself, though. And Noah. He would make it too. They both just had to.

I was so worried for Noah and Lizzie, and I was breaking down under the stress of this job that was never meant for me. I thought I was about to have a full-blown panic attack right there, sitting in a pile of fake snow.

Finally, some agents made their way over to me with a stretcher. "Okay Meg," the agent from earlier said to me. "We're just going to pick you up and put you on this stretcher here and carry you out now." She was talking very slowly and clearly, which was good because it was still hard for me to understand her.

My head was hurting more and more, and my thoughts were getting more and more muddled. I let them pick me up and carry me out into the way too bright sun. I had to close my eyes, it was so bright, and after I closed them, I couldn't get them to open again. I felt myself being loaded into an ambulance and be strapped down.

After a few minutes, I felt the car start and felt it start to move. It was finally over. I was leaving. The swaying of the car and the sound of the tires on the road coupled with my pounding head and my absolute exhaustion was enough to lure me right to sleep.

* * *

When I came to, I was at a hospital, laying in a bed, staring at the ceiling. I tried to look around, but that sent a shot of pain through my head. I reached my hand toward it and felt a big cotton bandage wrapping around my skull. Even touching the bandage made my head hurt.

From what I could see without moving my head, I was all alone in a hospital room painted a pretty sage green. There was a window on one wall, but the blinds were closed. There wasn't anything else in the room worth mentioning except for a small, pink balloon on my bedside table that read "Get Well Soon!" in big purple letters next to a cartoon cat. I started to wonder who it was from, but I didn't have to question it for long because the door to the room opened and in stepped Kat.

It was so good to see a friendly face that tears came to my eyes. Kat had become my family, and I was so thankful she was here. I desperately needed my family right now.

"How long have I been out?" I asked.

"About a day," she said. "How are you feeling?"

"Honestly," I started, "I feel . . . awful." I really didn't have words for what I was feeling. My head hurt so badly it was painful to think and I was so worried about Lizzie and Noah.

"Meg, I'm so sorry," Kat said. That surprised me. She had

been nothing but helpful throughout all of this; she had nothing to be sorry for.

"Why?" I asked.

"I shouldn't have pushed you as hard as I did into being a Keeper. It's clearly not you. It hurt you so much to do all that you did and I'm so sorry. It's just that being a Keeper has helped me so much and I was hoping it would help you."

She was blaming herself for getting me into this.

"No, Kat," I replied. "This isn't your fault at all. You're right, I'm definitely not meant to do it anymore, but it did help me at the beginning. Please don't blame yourself. You're like a sister to me and if anything good came out of all of this, it's that I met you."

"Oh, Meg," Kat said starting to tear up. She reached out for my hand, and we sat there, as almost-sisters for a few minutes before my worry took over again.

"How's Noah?" I asked, slightly afraid of the answer.

"He's in surgery right now," she said, sounding optimistic. "The doctors said they felt that he would most likely make it." Tears sprang to my eyes. Good tears this time. He was okay.

"What about Lizzie?" I asked, hoping for more good news.

Kat paused. "I'm so sorry Meg, but she . . . Lizzie didn't make it. She was gone before we made it to the hospital."

My tears started flowing. Sad tears. Lots of them. No. This couldn't be happening. Lizzie was gone? She really wasn't just sleeping. I sobbed, and Kat sat next to me, holding my hand. We stayed like that for a long time, until my tears dried up and I had nothing left to cry. But there was still a huge pit inside of me.

"I'm here for you," Kat said, sadly. "Let me know if there's anything I can do." I nodded, thankful for the sentiment, but I knew there was nothing she could do to fix the past.

47

Nolly

I sat in one of the hospital rooms, staring out the window. It was a nice day outside. There weren't any clouds and from the window, I could see a park. There was a little pond with ducks swimming around in it and a small playground. There were a few families there, some of them by the pond feeding the ducks and some of them over by the playground.

There was a little boy by the pond who would scream with delight every time one of the ducks took a bite of the bread his dad was holding. There was a couple on a park bench watching two little girls chase each other around the playground, smiling and laughing.

It was crazy how normal the outside world seemed when my world had completely fallen apart. I had no clue what was going to happen next and that terrified me. I could be sent to prison. I could be sent to reform school. I had no idea. One thing was for sure though: my old life was gone. Gone were the days of going to theater class and gossiping the whole time. Gone were the days where my biggest problem was not being able to find the right top to wear. Gone were the days of spending hours of my time fantasizing about boys. I was sure I wouldn't be able to do those things anymore.

But the funny thing was that that was okay with me. I didn't want to spend all my time thinking about gossip, fashion, and boys. I didn't want to be that stuck up, selfish girl that I was. And I was absolutely done with living to gain the attention of my parents. I wasn't going to let myself get carried away in trying to win their approval again. I wanted to change. I wanted to do some good in the world. I wanted to live in a way that would make Lizzie proud.

Just thinking about Lizzie brought tears to my eyes. The fact that she had still loved me when no one else did and that she had held onto our friendship even when I had done so much to ruin it made me realize how good of a friend she was.

And now she was gone. She had given up her life to save me. I was still in shock about it all. All I knew for sure was that I was going to use the life she had given me for good. And the first thing I was going to do was tell the agents the truth about everything that happened.

I knew that wasn't really a big thing to some, but it was to me. I was so used to living in lies, always trying to make myself seem better than I was, but I was done with that. I knew the agents would come talk to me at some point today, and when they did, I was ready to tell the truth.

Right after we had left the bunker, we came straight to the hospital. They had put me in one of the hospital rooms, but not really as a patient. They said they wanted to monitor my mental health, and the room had also been acting like a holding cell. I stayed there the rest of yesterday and slept there last night, having no idea what was going to happen.

Earlier this morning, a doctor had told me the agents would

check on me today and tell me what was going to happen. I was trying to distract myself until then, so I kept staring out the window, watching all the smiling people in the park.

Eventually, I heard a knock on my door.

"Come in," I said quietly. A few agents and some other government official type people came into my room. They all pulled up chairs near me and sat down. I was so nervous. My hands were shaking. Then, a girl with dirty blonde hair, light blue eyes, and a kind smile asked me to explain what had happened. The whole story, from start to finish.

Old habits die hard though because, for a second, I thought about lying, making up a story to try to get out of trouble. But then I thought about Lizzie and how she had saved me. I had to make her proud. I had to do the right thing. I told them the truth. The whole story, from my getting in the car with Cain to my being put in this hospital room. All the agents listened and wrote down some of what I said. By the time I was done, I was in tears. How had I messed up my life so badly? I desperately wanted a second chance. I needed one. And I promised myself, if I got one, I wouldn't waste it.

"Please don't send me to prison for the rest of my life," I said to the agents, desperately. "I know I messed up and that's probably what I deserve, but I want to change. I want to do better." The agents looked at one another, then the blonde woman spoke.

"Look, Nolly," she started. "Based on your story, it sounds like you didn't want to cause harm. You wanted to get attention from your parents, which is normal for girls your age. I'm not saying what you did was right, by any means, but I understand where you were coming from. Also, you were raised by parents whose lifestyle was crime. Again, not an excuse, but I get it.

We've also talked with Meg some, and she told us about Lizzie's dying wish. That we don't send you to prison. We want to honor Lizzie's wish, but we can't let you go without any consequences at all. We've decided that the best course of action it to let you finish high school in a reform-type school. You'll be with other girls your age who have gotten caught up in crime but want to change, and the school has a very supportive staff that I think will really help you. After that, you'll have a parole officer who you will need to check in with until we have decided you don't need that anymore."

Overwhelmed with gratitude, I started crying again. I wasn't going to prison. I was going to be surrounded by people who supported me and wanted me to be better. I was going to be able to start a new life. A better one.

"Thank you so much," I told the agents through my tears. "You won't regret this. I promise I'll do better."

"I know you will," said the blonde agent with a smile. Then, a doctor came in and made the agents leave, telling them that I needed my rest. The doctor asked me some questions about my mental health and how I was feeling. I told him I wasn't doing so hot. I was honest, not trying to pretend I was better than I was. And it felt so good. The doctor told me that I was going to meet with a therapist three times a week for at least the next month. Then, she said that I should probably get some rest and left.

Now that I knew what was going to happen in my future, I was able to relax. Suddenly, I was really tired. I lay down, thinking about all that had happened. Lizzie and the agents had given me a second chance. I was determined to not let Lizzie's sacrifice go to waste.

48

Meg

The next morning, Kat came into my room, and we sat in silence again. Today, they would know for sure about Noah. I was a huge, tangled mess of worry. I had been trying to sleep as much as possible to avoid thinking about it, but eventually, a person just can't sleep anymore. My head still hurt too bad for me to get up or watch anything on TV, so all I could do was stare at the ceiling, which made it was too easy for my thoughts to start drifting towards Noah.

Thankfully, Kat had been visiting me as much as she could, talking to me and giving me updates. She told me about Nolly and how she was going to reform school. I was glad she wasn't going to prison. I knew she made a lot of mistakes, but I still didn't want to see her suffer. And in the end, I could tell that she really did love Lizzie.

I was also trying to avoid thinking about Lizzie. I couldn't believe she was gone. I cried every time I thought about her. It was painful, but it felt good to get the tears out and not hold them in. And soon my tears for Lizzie would turn into worry-tears for Noah. Over and over. Sad about Lizzie and worried about Noah. Those two things constantly kept cycling through my mind. As I sat there, waiting for news, I caught Kat looking at me worriedly.

"What is it Kat?" I asked her, even though I knew why she was making that face.

"I'm just worried about you," she said. "This is so much for someone your age, well, any age, to handle."

"I'm-"

"No, don't say you're fine," Kat interrupted, knowing exactly what I was about to say. "You're definitely not fine. No one would be after going through what you went through."

"You're right Kat," I said surrendering. "I feel terrible. I feel like I failed Lizzie and Noah, and now Lizzie's gone, and I may never see Noah again. I never told you this but he and I used to be best friends, and I just need him to be okay so we can have that again."

"Oh, Meg," Kat said. "You know none of this is your fault, right?"

I nodded. I knew that was true, but I was still having a hard time convincing myself that it was.

"And as far as Noah goes, the doctors said he will probably be okay. We will find out soon, but until then I'm here if you need to scream or cry or vent or if you want me to go sneak in some ice cream from the hospital cafeteria, I can do that too."

"Thanks, Kat," I said with a small smile on my lips. "For now, though, can we just sit?"

"Absolutely." We sat there in silence, waiting. And waiting. Finally, a doctor came in, bringing the news we were waiting for.

"He made it through the surgery," she said. "He's going to be fine. He should be waking up soon."

Kat jumped out of her chair, and I felt myself break into a grin. He was alive! He was alive! I was going to get to see him! I was going to get to thank him for all he had done to help me! And we would get to rekindle our friendship . . . and maybe at some point make it more than that.

The doctor loaded me into a wheelchair, and we went to Noah's room. Noah was laying in the bed hooked up to a bunch of machines looking pretty beat up. But the heart monitor next to his bed was keeping a steady beat and I could see his chest rising and falling. That was all I cared about. Kat sat down next to me, and we waited. And waited.

Until, "Hey, glad to see you're alive too."

"Noah!" I screamed with the biggest smile on my face. I leaned over to give him a hug, so happy that I had the chance to. He was alive. I talked to Noah for a while, me holding his hand, him smiling back at me until the doctors forced me to leave so Noah could rest. I was so thankful that he made it. I was still so, so sad about Lizzie, and I knew that I probably always would be, but at least I had Noah to go through the grief with me.

49

Noah

Meg and I spent a lot of time together over the next few days. We told each other what it was like being on opposite sides of the story. I told her how Nolly had betrayed us, and she told me how Lizzie had died to save Nolly. I was shocked and depressed by the news. I couldn't believe that Lizzie was gone. We had been through so much together over the past few weeks. I wouldn't have made it through this disaster without her. And now she was gone. Why I had made it and she didn't was something I would never understand. Her forgiveness to Nolly also amazed me. She gave her life to a girl who betrayed her. I guess she still loved her best friend even though she had messed up. It would take me a while to forgive Nolly, but if that's what Lizzie did and that's what she wanted, then I would do it too. For Lizzie. I would miss her for a long time, but I had Meg, and we were working through our grief together.

A few days later, once Meg was walking (her concussion had been pretty serious) and I could get around in a wheelchair, the agents called a meeting with us. There were two people there:

someone they called "the director" and Kat, who I had gotten to know over the past week. Meg had said she was like her big sister and that she was the one who had helped and supported her through the case. If she was a friend of Meg's, then she was a friend of mine. For our meeting though, the director did most of the talking.

"First of all," he started. "I want to thank you all for helping us to catch these criminals. You were both very brave. Today, I want to fill you in on all the gaps, so please, don't be scared to ask questions. As you may or may not have guessed or known, Cain was trying to restart his father's counterfeit ring. That was what all the money & machinery was for in the bunker. Cain first had to get the instruction manual at the first house and the key at the second. While at the bunker, he kidnapped Meg and drove away, knowing he'd be able to go back later. Our agents called for reinforcements and medics, but they didn't make it before the bomb was set off by Cain's henchmen. They did make it in time, however, for when Cain came to the bunker a second time. He was shooting anyone who got close to him except for Nolly because she was working with him. However, he turned on her at the last second and went to shoot her, but Lizzie jumped in the way and took the bullet, saving Nolly's life. We then were engaged in a shootout between our men and Cain, which ended in Cain's death. Then, we drove you two and Nolly to the hospital. Lizzie, unfortunately, did not make it before we arrived. Noah, you, thankfully, pulled through your surgery and, Meg, you only had your concussion and small injuries. As did Nolly. Because of Nolly's age, her level of involvement, and Lizzie's last wish for her to not go to prison, Nolly will finish out high school in reform school. Then, she will most likely be out on parole for a few years. She is seeing a therapist right now, but it's been very clear to all the doctors and agents that have talked to her that she is trying to turn her life around."

He paused, giving it a second to sink in.

"I know that was a lot of information, but that about sums it up."

Wow, was all I could think. It was a lot to take in. I already knew most of that, but hearing someone else tell me the story showed me just how much we had been through. These past few weeks of my life had been crazy. It had been absolutely terrible, but at least now it was over. And good had won over evil. Like it always does. I was still thinking through everything when the director spoke again.

"Do either of you have any questions?" he asked. My brain was still trying to process, but I did have one question.

"What happens to us now?" I asked, ready to go back to my normal life.

"Well," the director started, "It's kind of up to you. Once you're cleared by the hospital, you could go back to your old school and finish out the year, you could finish the year in online classes, or you could take the rest of the year off and restart the next school year."

I thought about that. What did I want to do? I had just been through so much, but I didn't really feel like hiding from reality would do me any good. If I went back, people would ask me all sorts of questions and, while I didn't want to relive everything that happened, I also didn't want to pretend like nothing had happened at all. Everything I'd been through had been terrible, but it had made me stronger and more courageous.

"I want to go back to my old school," I told the director firmly.

"OK, then," he said. "As soon as the hospital clears you, we will make sure you are re-enrolled and all set to go." I nodded my thanks, getting emotional about finally returning to school and normal life. There were times in the past few weeks I wasn't sure I would get to.

"What about me?" Meg asked, drawing my attention back to her. "I can't be a Keeper anymore. What am I going to do?"

"Well, Meg," Kat started. "I've been thinking about this. How would you feel about coming to live with me? You could finish school online and just hang at my place until you're ready for college in about a year. Plus, I live close enough to your old school you could still see your friends on the weekends. What do you think?" Kat looked a little nervous, but Meg was beaming.

"Really?" she asked. "You want me to live with you?"

"Of course! If you want to," Kat said, starting to smile at Meg's excitement.

"Are you kidding? I would love to!" Meg said with a huge grin on her face. It was good to see her smile. Especially after the nightmare we had been through.

"It's all settled then," the director said, also smiling. I grabbed Meg's hand and smiled at her.

"It's finally over," she said, and I could see the weight of the past few weeks lift off her shoulders. Then Kat spoke.

"I'm so very proud of you two. You both played a major part in stopping Cain. Most kids your age would have frozen and accepted defeat. But not you. You stood up against the evil. And won. I couldn't be prouder."

50

5 years later: Meg

I'm sitting in our coffee shop, staring out the window. The leaves are turning yellow and orange and staring to fall. As people walk by, the leaves scurry across the pavement. Downtown is busy today. People walk back and forth, talking and laughing. Across the street is a boutique full of homecoming dresses, and I watch as the girls go in, hoping to find the perfect dress, then come out carrying their treasures. There's a man on the corner selling hot apple cider, and there's a line of people waiting their turn to buy the treat.

All in all, it's a peaceful, happy scene. Which is good, because today is a hard day. Five years ago today, Lizzie died. We all miss her terribly, and I don't think that will ever really go away. We just have to learn how to live life to the fullest in her absence, reminding ourselves it's what she would have wanted. Every year since she died, Noah, Nolly, and I have made it a point to meet on this day. To remember everything that happened and to help each other through it. It took Noah and me a little while to forgive Nolly, but we both knew it's what Lizzie wanted and that was really all the persuasion we needed.

"Hey," Noah says, returning from the bathroom in the back of the café. He sits in the booth next to me and slides his arm across my shoulders. We started dating about six months after everything calmed down, and we've been together almost five years.

Noah truly is one of the best parts of my life. He is kind, funny, strong, and he always finds a way to bring me joy when I start feeling depressed. After we finished high school, we went to Boston University together. We met lots of new people and had the time of our lives. We got to hang out together a lot, but we also got to hang out with our new friends. We went to the football games and the theater performances and all the other college events. We also did lots of homework and studying.

We had this spot in the park across from the college where we went all the time. There's a big tree with huge branches that stretch all the way out to cover the path. Across from it, there's a little pond that has a family of ducks living in it. Under the tree, there's a picnic table where we would study, write papers, and eat lunch. We spent lots of time working under that tree, and it finally paid off. We both graduated in May and now Noah is going to med school and I'm going to vet school. We are both getting to follow our dreams.

And not just our career dreams either. Last weekend, Noah and I went out to dinner at a really nice restaurant. There was live music and fancy silverware and a Maitre d' and everything. After dinner, we walked through the park until we got to our favorite part of Boston. Our tree. At night, there are lights in the tree that shine down through its leaves and cast little shadows all around. It's beautiful. When we got there, Noah knelt down and pulled out a ring, asking me to marry him. I said. "Yes," so happy I could barely think.

Now, as we are sitting in the café waiting for Nolly, the beautiful ring he gave me is catching the rays of the autumn sun, making it sparkle even more. I look out the window again, just in time to see Nolly walking up. The bell above the door tinkles as she walks in.

"Hi, guys!" she says. "I'm so sorry I'm late. There was a situation as the shelter I had to take care of."

"Oh, no worries," I say, smiling at her. Out of all of us, Nolly has changed the most. She truly turned her life around. She currently works at a women's shelter, helping women escape abusive home lives. She created a program there that focuses on helping girls whose parents aren't there for them have a place to turn to. She loves her job, and I know it makes her feel fulfilled that she gets to help women who are in similar situations at home that she used to be in.

"I saw your big news!!" Nolly squeals, pointing at my ring as she slides into the seat across from Noah and me. "I'm so excited for the two of you!"

"Thank you, Nolly!" I say beaming, showing her my ring that's still sparkling in the sun.

"It's just perfect!" she says. "Just like the two of you!"

"Oh, Nolly," Noah says, shaking his head, but grinning from ear to ear.

"So, when's the wedding?" Nolly asks excitedly. Noah shakes his head again, but he's laughing at how excited she is for us. Nolly really and truly is the most supportive friend.

"We aren't sure yet," I say, "But there is something related to the wedding I need to ask you about," I say to her.

"Oh, what is it?" Nolly asks, her excitement continuing to build.

"Will you be my Maid of Honor? You're my best friend and

the most supportive person I know. I wouldn't want anyone else right by me on my wedding day."

"Oh, Meg," Nolly says, starting to tear up. "Of course, I will. I would love to."

I smile at her, taking her hand and squeezing it. I lean my head on Noah's shoulder and close my eyes, smiling, thankful for the friends I have beside me, and the future I have ahead of me. Especially when there was a time I almost lost both.

Author's Note: Why Did Lizzie Have to Die?

Hi, readers! If you're reading this, I just want to say THANK YOU! Thank you for picking up my book and reading it! You mean the world to me! Before you put this book down, there is just one more thing I want to say. I want to explain why Lizzie had to die.

First of all, this book isn't just a good story about four characters going on an adventure. This book is a representation of something much, much bigger: the story of you, me, and a guy called Jesus. I am a Christian, a believer in Jesus, and Jesus is the most important part of my life. When I was writing this book, I knew I wanted the story of Jesus to be represented.

You see, each and every one of us makes mistakes, called sins. We lie, we cheat, we're rude to those around us, we break the rules, and we just mess up in general. The sad part is that these mistakes separate us from God, our loving father and creator. When God created us, he created us to be in a relationship with him, but our mistakes make that relationship impossible because God is perfect, and he can't be in the presence of sin. Just like Nolly's mistakes were separating her from Lizzie, our sins separate us from God.

A price has to be paid for our sins. They must be punished. The price for our sins is death. Eternal death and separation from God in Hell. I know this sounds pretty dark, but I promise you, it gets better.

Because God loves us and doesn't want us to be separated from him, he came up with a plan. He sent his perfect Son, Jesus, fully God and fully man, to live on Earth. Jesus lived a perfect life, never making any mistakes. Then, Jesus died on the cross, taking the punishment for our sins on him. Just like Lizzie died to save Nolly, Jesus died to save you and me. But unlike Lizzie, Jesus didn't stay dead. He rose from the grave three days later, showing he had defeated sin and death.

Just like Lizzie forgave Nolly for all that she had done, we can be forgiven for all the wrongs we have done too. If you believe that Jesus, the Son of God, died on the cross and rose from the dead to forgive you from your sins, you can be saved. Once you make this decision, you are saved! Your sins are forgiven, and you can begin a relationship with God. Not only that, but when you die, you will get to spend eternity with our Father in Heaven. Believing in Jesus is the only way. You can't be forgiven by doing enough good things or believing in other gods, only Jesus.

It is my hope and prayer that each and every one of my readers chooses to believe in Jesus. I promise, it is the best decision you could ever make! If you do make this decision, I encourage you to reach out! Find another Christian, visit a church, or start reading a Bible! Begin your journey with Jesus and never look back!

Acknowledgments

First of all, I want to thank Jesus, my rock and my redeemer, for all he has done for me. I want to thank him most of all for sacrificing his life for me. If you want to know more about what I'm talking about, I encourage you to check out the Author's Note. I also want to thank him for giving me the creativity and drive to complete this project. I could never have done it without him.

Second, I want to thank my amazing, fantastic, crazy-awesome family. Ever since I was little, I wanted to write a book and they constantly encouraged me in that dream. Thank you to my parents for teaching me that the sky's the limit and that I can do anything I put my mind to. Thank you to Glory and Luke for always making me laugh and constantly inspiring me. Thanks for encouraging me along this journey, asking how the book was going, and letting me ask random questions about what to write.

Thank you to my awesome friends who thought it was so cool when I said I was writing a book. Thanks for going along with all my craziness and wild ideas. Y'all really are the best friends a gal could ask for.

Thank you to the awesome youth leaders and YoungLife leaders I've gotten to meet and learn from over the years. Y'all have helped me grow so much as a person and in my faith, and I am so grateful for y'all.

Thank you to all the awesome teachers I've had who not only taught me how to write but instilled in me a love for the subject. Thank you for giving up so much to teach me and my fellow students. Y'all are amazing.

Thank you to Barbie Bowen for doing an amazing job editing my book. I'm so thankful I found you, and I appreciate not only your awesome edits but your prayers for my book to bring others to Christ.

Thank you to Kimberly Stambaugh for designing a stunning cover. You perfectly captured what I wanted, and I love it so much. Thanks for going along with all my little edits and working with me until we got something perfect.

Lastly, thanks to you, my amazing reader. Thank you for choosing this book and for reading it all the way through. Without you, I wouldn't get to be the author I am, so I thank you so much for that. I hope you enjoyed going on an adventure with Lizzie, Noah, Meg, and Nolly, and I hope you learned something more about God and his great love for us. Again, thank you for reading my book. You are amazing!

About the Author

A Texas native, Grace is a passionate writer excited about publishing her debut novel. Her other passions involve reading, dancing, and spending time with her friends, family, and golden retriever, Howdy. She is a dedicated follower of Christ, and enjoys her local YoungLife and youth ministry. She also enjoys spending time outdoors, hanging out on the lake, and hiking. Some of her other favorite things are iced coffee, rain, Birkenstocks, and sweatshirts. She is currently a high school student, and she plans on graduating in 2024 and attending Texas A&M University.

9 798218 302832